Start Publishing PD is a registered trademark of Start Publishing PD LLC
Manufactured in the United States of America

Cover art: Shutterstock/Taisiya Kozorez

Cover design: Jennifer Do

10 9 8 7 6 5 4 3 2 1

ISBN 979-8-8809-1461-6

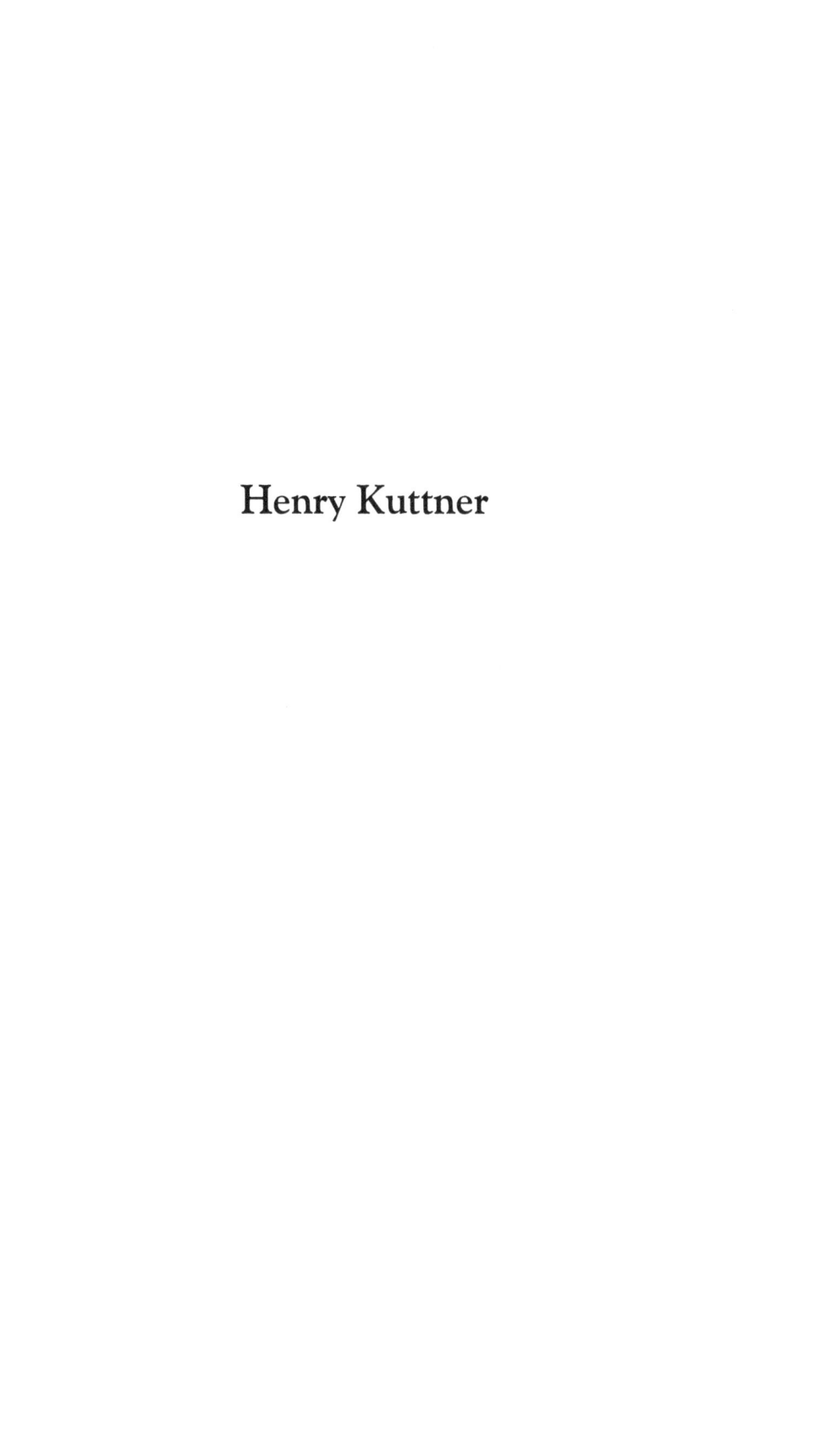

Henry Kuttner

Table of Contents

To the north thin smoke made a column against the darkening sky. Again I felt the unreasoning fear, the impulse toward nightmare flight that had been with me for a long time now. I knew it was without reason. There was only smoke, rising from the swamps of the tangled Limberlost country, not fifty miles from Chicago, where man has outlawed superstition with strong bonds of steel and concrete.

I knew it was only a camper's fire, yet *I knew it was not*. Something, far back in my mind, knew what the smoke rose from, and who stood about the fire, peering my way through the trees.

I looked away, my glance slipping around the crowded walls— shelves bearing the random fruit of my uncle's magpie collector's instinct. Opium pipes of inlaid work and silver, golden chessmen from India, a sword . . .

Deep memories stirred within me—deep panic. I was beneath the sword in two strides, tearing it from the wall, my fingers cramping hard around the hilt. Not fully aware of what I did, I found myself facing the window and the distant smoke again. The sword was in my fist, but feeling wrong, not reassuring, not as *the* sword ought to feel.

"Easy, Ed," my uncle's deep voice said behind me. "What's the matter? You look—sort of wild."

"It's the wrong sword," I heard myself saying helplessly.

Then something like a mist cleared from my brain. I blinked at him stupidly, wondering what was happening to me. My voice answered.

"It isn't the sword. It should have come from Cambodia. It should have been one of the three talismans of the Fire King and the Water King. Three very great talismans—the fruit of *cui*, gathered at the time of the deluge, but still fresh—the rattan with flowers that never fade, and the sword of Yan, the guarding spirit."

My uncle squinted at me through pipe-smoke. He shook his head.

"You've changed, Ed," he said in his deep, gentle voice. "You've changed a lot. I suppose because of the war—it's to be expected. And you've been sick. But you never used to be interested in things like that before. I think you spend too much time at the libraries. I'd hoped this vacation would help. The rest—"

"I don't want rest!" I said violently. "I spent a year and a half resting in Sumatra. Doing nothing but rest in that smelly little jungle village, waiting and waiting and waiting."

I could see and smell it now. I could feel again the fever that had raged so long through me as I lay in the tabooed hut.

My mind went back eighteen months to the last hour when things were normal for me. It was in the closing phases of World War II, and I was flying over the Sumatran jungle. War, of course, is never good or normal, but until that one blinding moment in the air I had been an ordinary man, sure of myself, sure of my place in the world, with no nagging fragments of memory too elusive to catch.

Then everything blanked out, suddenly and completely. I never knew what it was. There was nothing it could have been. My only injuries came when the plane struck, and they were miraculously light. But I had been whole and unhurt when the blindness and blankness came over me.

The friendly Bataks found me as I lay in the ruined plane. They brought me through a fever and a raging illness with their strange, crude, effective ways of healing, but I sometimes thought they had done me no service when they saved me. And their witchdoctor had his doubts, too.

He knew something. He worked his curious, futile charms with knotted string and rice, sweating with effort I did not understand—then. I remembered the scarred, ugly mask looming out of the shadow, the hands moving in gestures of strange power.

"Come back, O soul, where thou are lingering in the wood, or in the hills, or by the river. See, I call thee with a *toemba bras*, with an egg of the fowl Rajah *moelija*, with the eleven healing leaves . . . ."

Yes, they were sorry for me at first, all of them. The witchdoctor was the first to sense something wrong, and the awareness spread. I could feel it spreading, as their attitude changed. They were afraid. Not of me, I thought, but of—of what?

Before the helicopter came to take me back to civilization, the witch-doctor told me a little. As much, perhaps, as he dared.

"You must hide, my son. All your life you must hide. Something is searching for you—" He used a word I did not understand. "—and it has come from the Other World, the ghostlands, to hunt you down. Remember this: all magic things must be taboo to you. And if that too fails, perhaps you may find a weapon in magic. But we cannot help you. Our powers are not strong enough for that."

He was glad to see me go. They were all glad.

And after that, unrest. For something had changed me utterly. The fever? Perhaps. At any rate, I didn't feel like the same man. There were dreams, memories—haunting urgencies as if I had somehow, somewhere left some vital job unfinished . . ..

I found myself talking more freely to my uncle.

"It was like a curtain lifting. A curtain of gauze. I saw some things more clearly—they seemed to have a different significance. Things happen to me now that would have seemed incredible—before. Now they don't.

"I've traveled a lot, you know. It doesn't help. There's always something to remind me. An amulet in a pawnshop window, a knotted string, a cat's-eye opal and two figures. It see them in my dreams, over and over. And once—"

I stopped.

"Yes?" my uncle prompted softly.

"It was in New Orleans. I woke up one night and there was something in my room, very close to me. I had a gun—a special sort of gun—under my pillow. When I reached for it the—call it a dog—sprang from the window. Only it wasn't shaped quite like a dog." I hesitated. "There were silver bullets in the revolver," I said.

My uncle was silent for a long moment. I knew what he was thinking.

"The other figure?" he said, finally.

"I don't know. It wears a hood. I think it's very old. And beyond these two—"

"Yes?"

"A voice. A very sweet voice, haunting. A fire. And beyond the fire, a face I have never seen clearly."

My uncle nodded. The darkness had drawn in; I could scarcely see him, and the smoke outside had lost itself against the shadow of night. But a faint glow still lingered beyond the trees . . . or did I only imagine that?

I nodded toward the window.

"I've seen that fire before," I told him.

"What's wrong with it? Campers make fires."

"No. It's a Need-fire."

"What the devil is that?"

"It's a ritual," I said. "Like the Midsummer fires, or the Beltane fire the Scots used to kindle. But the Need-fire is lighted only in time of calamity. It's a very old custom."

My uncle laid down his pipe and leaned forward.

"What is it, Ed? Do you have any inkling at all?"

"Psychologically I suppose you could call it a persecution complex," I said slowly. "I—believe in things I never used to. I think someone is trying to find me—has found me. And is calling. Who it is I don't know. What they want I don't know. But a little while ago I found out one more thing—this sword."

I picked the sword up from the table.

"It isn't what I want," I went on, "but sometimes, when my mind is—abstract, something from outside floats into it. Like the need for a sword. And not any sword—just one. I don't know what the sword looks like, but I'd know if I held it in my hand." I laughed a little. "And if I drew it a few inches from the sheath, I could put out that fire up there as if I'd blown on it like a candle-flame. And if I drew the sword all the way out—the world would come to an end!"

My uncle nodded. After a moment, he spoke.

"The doctors," he asked. "What do they say?"

"I know what they would say, if I told them," I said grimly. "Pure insanity. If I could be sure of that, I'd feel happier. One of the dogs was killed last night, you know."

"Of course. Old Duke. Another dog from some farm, eh?"

"Or a wolf. The same wolf that got into my room last night, and stood over me like a man, and clipped off a lock of my hair."

Something flamed up far away, beyond the window, and was gone in the dark. The Need-fire.

My uncle rose and stood looking down at me in the dimness. He laid a big hand on my shoulder.

"I think you're sick, Ed."

"You think I'm crazy. Well, I may be. But I've got a hunch I'm going to know soon, one way or the other."

I picked up the sheathed sword and laid it across my knees. We sat in silence for what seemed like a long time.

In the forest to the north, the Need-fire burned steadily. I could not see it. But its flames stirred in my blood—dangerously— darkly.

I could not sleep. The suffocating breathlessness of the late summer lay like a woollen blanket over me. Presently I went into the big room and restlessly searched for cigarettes. My uncle's voice came through an open doorway.

"All right, Ed?"

"Yeah. I can't sleep yet. Maybe I'll read."

I chose a book at random, sank into a relaxer chair, and switched on a lamp. It was utterly silent. I could not even hear the faint splashing of little waves on the lakeshore.

There was something I wanted—

A trained rifleman's hand, at need, will itch for the familiar feeling of smooth wood and metal. Similarly, my hand was hungry for the feel of something—neither gun nor sword, I thought. A weapon that I had used before. I could not remember what it was. Once I glanced at the poker leaning against the fireplace, and thought that was it; but the flash of recognition was gone instantly.

The book was a popular novel. I skimmed through it rapidly. The dim, faint, pulsing in my blood did not wane. It grew stronger, rising from sub-sensory levels. A distant excitement seemed to be growing deep in my mind.

Grimacing, I rose to return the book to its shelf. I stood there for a moment, my glance skimming over the titles. On impulse I drew out a volume I had not looked at for many years, the Book of Common Prayer.

It fell open in my hands. A sentence blazed out from the page.

I am become as it were a monster unto many.

I put back the book and returned to my chair. I was in no mood for reading. The lamp overhead bothered me, and I pressed the switch. Instantly moonlight flooded the room—and instantly the curious sense of expectancy was heightened, as though I had lowered a—a barrier.

The sheathed sword still lay on the window-seat. I looked past it, to the clouded sky where a golden moon shone. Faint, far away, a glimmer showed—the Need-fire, blazing in the swampy wilderness of the Limberlost.

And it called.

The golden square of window was hypnotic. I lay back in my chair, half-closing my eyes, while the sense of danger moved coldly within my brain. Sometimes before I had felt this call, summoning me. And always before I had been able to resist.

This time I wavered.

The lock of hair clipped from my head—had that given the enemy power? Superstition. My logic called it that, but a deep, inner well of conviction told me that the ancient hair-magic was not merely mummery. Since that time in Sumatra I had been far less skeptical. And since then I had studied.

The studies were strange enough, ranging from the principles of sympathetic magic to the wild fables of lycanthropy and de-monology. Yet I was amazingly quick at learning.

It was as though I took a refresher course, to remind myself of knowledge I had once known by heart. Only one subject really troubled me, and I continually stumbled across it, by roundabout references.

And that was the Force, the entity, disguised in folklore under such familiar names as the Black Man, Satan, Lucifer, and such unfamiliar names as Kutchie, of the Australian Dieris, Tuña, of the Esquimaux, the African Abonsam, and the Swiss Strätteli.

I did no research on the Black Man—but I did not need to. There was a recurrent dream that I could not help identifying with the dark force that represented evil. I would be standing before a golden square of light, very much afraid, and yet straining toward some consummation that I desired. And deep down within that glowing square there would be the beginning of motion. I knew there were certain ritual gestures to be made before the ceremony could be begun, but it was difficult to break the paralysis that held me.

A square like the moon-drenched window before me—yet not the same.

For no chill essence of fear thrust itself out at me now. Rather, the low humming I heard was soothing, gentle as a woman's crooning voice.

The golden square wavered—shook—and little tendrils of crepuscular light fingered out toward me. Ever the low humming came, alluring and disarming.

Golden fingers—tentacles—they darted here and there as if puzzled. They touched lamp, table, carpet, and drew back. They—touched me.

Swiftly they leaped forward now—avid! I had time for a momentary pulse of alarm before they wrapped me in an embrace like golden sands of sleep. The humming grew louder. And I responded to it.

As the skin of the flayed satyr Marsyas thrilled at the sound of his native Phrygian melodies! I knew this music. I knew this—chant!

Stole through the golden glow a crouching shadow—not human—with amber eyes and a bristling mane—the shadow of a wolf.

It hesitated, glanced over its shoulder questioningly. And now another shape swam into view, cowled and gowned so that nothing of its face or body showed. But it was small—small as a child.

Wolf and cowled figure hung in the golden mists, watching and waiting. The sighing murmur altered. Formed itself into syllables and words. Words in no human tongue, but—I knew them.

"Ganelon! I call you, Ganelon! By the seal in your blood—hear me!"

Ganelon! Surely that was my name. I knew it so well.

Yet who called me thus?

"I have called you before, but the way was not open. Now the bridge is made. Come to me Ganelon!"

A sigh.

The wolf glanced over a bristling shoulder, snarling. The cowled figure bent toward me. I sensed keen eyes searching me from the darkness of the hood, and an icy breath touched me.

"He has forgotten, Medea," said a sweet, high-pitched voice, like the tone of a child.

Again the sigh. "Has he forgotten me? Ganelon, Ganelon! Have you forgotten the arms of Medea, the lips of Medea?"

I swung, cradled in the golden mists, half asleep.

"He has forgotten," the cowled figure said,

"Then let him come to me nevertheless. Ganelon! The Need-fire burns. The gateway lies open to the Dark World. By fire and earth, air and darkness, I summon you! Ganelon!"

"He has forgotten."

"Bring him. We have the power, now."

The golden sands thickened. Flame-eyed, wolf and robed shadow swam toward me. I felt myself lifted—moving forward, not of my own volition.

The window swung wide. I saw the sword, sheathed and ready. I snatched up the weapon, but I could not resist that relentless tide that carried me forward. Wolf and whispering shadow drifted with me.

"To the Fire. Bring him to the Fire."

"He has forgotten, Medea."

"To the Fire, Edeyrn. To the Fire."

Twisted tree-limbs floated past me. Far ahead I saw a flicker. It grew larger, nearer. It was the Need-fire.

Faster the tide bore me. Toward the fire itself—

Not to Caer Llyr!

From the depths of my mind the cryptic words spewed. Amber-eyed wolf whirled to glare at me; cowled shadow swept in closer on the golden stream. I felt a chill of deadly cold drive through the curling mists.

"Caer Llyr," the cloaked Edeyrn whispered in the child's sweet voice. "He remembers Caer Llyr—but does he remember Llyr?"

"He will remember! He has been sealed to Llyr. And, in Caer Llyr, the Place of Llyr, he will remember."

The Need-fire was a towering pillar a few yards away. I fought against the dragging tide.

I lifted my sword—threw the sheath away. I cut at the golden mists that fettered me.

Under the ancient steel the shinning fog-wraiths shuddered and were torn apart—and drew back. There was a break in the humming harmony; for an instant, utter silence.

Then—

"Matholch!" the invisible whisperer cried. "Lord Matholch!"

The wolf crouched, fangs bared. I aimed a cut at its snarling mask. It avoided the blow easily and sprang.

It caught the blade between its teeth and wrenched the hilt from my grip.

The golden fogs surged back, folding me in their warm embrace.

"Caer Llyr," they murmured.

The Need-fire roared up in a scarlet fountain.

"Caer Llyr!" the flames shouted.

And out of those fires rose—a woman!

Hair dark as midnight fell softly to her knees. Under level brows she flashed one glance at me, a glance that held question and a fierce determination. She was loveliness incarnate. Dark loveliness.

Lilith. Medea, witch of Colchis!

And—

"The gateway closes," the child-voice of Edeyrn said.

The wolf, still mouthing my sword, crouched uneasily. But the woman of the fire said no word.

She held out her arms to me.

The golden clouds thrust me forward, into those white arms.

Wolf and cowled shadow sprang to flank us. The humming rose to a deep-pitched roar—a thunder as of crashing worlds.

"It is difficult, difficult," Medea said. "Help me, Edeyrn. Lord Matholch."

The fires died. Around us was not the moonlit wilderness of the Limberlost, but empty grayness, a featureless grayness that stretched to infinity. Not even stars showed against that blank.

And now there was fear in the voice of Edeyrn.

"Medea. I have not the—power. I stayed too long in the Earth-world."

"Open the gate!" Medea cried. "Thrust it open but a little way, or we stay here between the worlds forever!"

The wolf crouched, snarling. I felt energy pouring out of his beast-body. His brain that was not the brain of a beast.

Around us the golden clouds were dissipating.

The grayness stole in.

"Ganelon," Medea said. "Ganelon! Help me!"

A door in my mind opened. A formless darkness stole in.

I felt that deadly, evil shadow creep through me, and submerge my mind under ebon waves.

"He has the power," Edeyrn murmured. "He was sealed to Llyr. Let him call on—Llyr."

"No. No. I dare not. Llyr?" But Medea's face was turned to me questioningly.

At my feet the wolf snarled and strained, as though by sheer brute strength it might wrench open a gateway between locked worlds.

Now the black sea submerged me utterly. My thought reached out and was repulsed by the dark horror of sheer infinity, stretched forth again and—

Touched—something!

Llyr . . .*Llyr!*

"The gateway opens," Edeyrn said.

The gray emptiness was gone. Golden clouds thinned and vanished. Around me, white pillars rose to a vault far, far above. We stood on a raised dais upon which curious designs were emblazoned.

The tide of evil which had flowed through me had vanished.

But, sick with horror and self-loathing, I dropped to my knees, one arm shielding my eyes.

I had called on—*Llyr!*

Aching in every muscle, I woke and lay motionless, staring at the low ceiling. Memory flooded back. I turned my head, realizing that I lay on a soft couch padded with silks and pillows. Across the bare, simply furnished room was a recessed window, translucent, for it admitted light, but I could see only vague blurs through it.

Seated beside me, on a three-legged stool, was the dwarfed, robed figure I knew was Edeyrn.

Not even now could I see the face; the shadows within the cowl were too deep. I felt the keen glint of a watchful gaze, though, and a breath of something unfamiliar—cold and deadly. The robes were saffron, an ugly hue that held nothing of life in the harsh folds. Staring, I saw that the creature was less than four feet tall, or would have been had it stood upright.

Again I heard that sweet, childish, sexless voice.

"Will you drink, Lord Ganelon? Or eat?"

I threw back the gossamer robe covering me and sat up. I was wearing a thin tunic of silvery softness, and trunks of the same material. Edeyrn apparently had not moved, but a drapery swung apart in the wall, and a man came silently in, bearing a covered tray.

Sight of him was reassuring. He was a big man, sturdily muscled, and under a plumed Etruscan-styled helmet his face was tanned and strong. I thought so till I met his eyes. They were blue pools in which horror had drowned. And ancient fear, so familiar that it was almost submerged, lay deep in his gaze.

Silently he served me and in silence withdrew.

Edeyrn nodded toward the tray.

"Eat and drink. You will be stronger, Lord Ganelon."

There were meats and breads, of a sort, and a glass of colorless liquid that was not water, as I found on sampling it. I took a sip, set down the chalice, and scowled at Edeyrn.

"I gather that I'm not insane," I said.

"You are not. Your soul has been elsewhere—*you* have been in exile—but you are home again now."

"In Caer Llyr?" I asked, without quite knowing why.

Edeyrn shook the saffron robes.

"No. But you must remember?"

"I remember nothing. Who are you? What's happened to me?"

"You know that you are Ganelon?"

"My name's Edward Bond."

"Yet you almost remembered—at the Need-fire," Edeyrn said. "This will take time. And there is danger always. Who am I? I am Edeyrn—who serves the Coven."

"Are you—"

"A woman," she said, in that childish, sweet voice, laughing a little. "A very old woman, the oldest of the Coven. It has shrunk from its original thirteen. There is Medea, of course, Lord Matholch—" I remembered the wolf "—Ghast Rhymi, who has more power than any of us, but is too old to use it. And you, Lord Ganelon, or Edward Bond, as you name yourself. Five of us in all now. Once there were hundreds, but even I cannot remember that time, though Ghast Rhymi can, if he would."

I put my head in my hands.

"Good heavens, I don't know! Your words mean nothing to me. I don't even know where I am!"

"Listen," she said, and I felt a soft touch on my shoulder. "You must understand this. You have lost your memories."

"That's not true."

"It *is* true, Lord Ganelon. Your true memories were erased, and you were given artificial ones. All you think you recall now, of your life on the Earth-world—all that is false. It did not happen. At least, not to you."

"The Earth-world? I'm not on Earth?"

"This is a different world," she said. "But it is your own world. You came from here originally. The Rebels, our enemies, exiled you and changed your memories."

"That's impossible."

"Come here," Edeyrn said, and went to the window. She touched something, and the pane grew transparent. I looked over her shrouded head at a landscape I had never seen before.

Or had I?

Under a dull, crimson sun the rolling forest below lay bathed in bloody light. I was looking down from a considerable height, and could not make out details, but it seemed to me that the trees were oddly shaped and that they were moving. A river ran toward distant hills. A few white towers rose from the forest. That was all. Yet the scarlet, huge sun had told me enough. This was not the Earth I knew.

"Another planet?"

"More than that," she said. "Few in the Dark World know this. But *I* know—and there are some others who have learned, unluckily for you. There are worlds of probability, divergent in the stream of time, but identical almost, until the branches diverge too far."

"I don't understand that."

"Worlds coexistent in time and space—but separated by another dimension, the variant of probability. This is the world that might have been yours had *something* not happened, long ago. Originally the Dark World and the Earth-world were one, in space and time. Then a decision was made—a very vital decision, though I am not sure what it was. From that point the time-stream branched, and two variant worlds existed where there had been only one before.

"They were utterly identical at first, except that in one of them the key decision had not been made. The results were very different. It happened hundreds of years ago, but the two variant worlds are still close together in the time stream. Eventually they will drift farther apart, and grow less like each other. Meanwhile, they *are* similar, so much so that a man on the Earth-world may have his twin in the Dark World."

"His twin?"

"The man he might have been, had the key decision not been made ages ago in his world. Yes, twins, Ganelon—Edward Bond. Do you understand now?"

I returned to the couch and sat there, frowning.

"Two worlds, coexistent. I can understand that, yes. But I think you mean more—that a double for me exists somewhere."

"You were born in the Dark World. Your double, the true Edward Bond, was born on Earth. But we have enemies here, woodrunners, rebels, and they have stolen enough knowledge to bridge the gulf between time-variants. We ourselves learned the method only lately, though once it was well-known here, among the Coven.

"The rebels reached out across the gulf and sent you—sent Ganelon—into the Earth-world, so that Edward Bond could come here, among them. They—"

"But why?" I interrupted. "What reason could they have for that?"

Edeyrn turned her hooded head toward me, and I felt, not for the first time, a strange, remote chill as she fixed her unseen gaze upon my face.

"What reason?" she echoed in her sweet, cool voice. "Think, Ganelon. See if you remember."

I thought. I closed my eyes and tried to submerge my conscious mind, to let the memories of Ganelon rise up to that surface if they were there at all. I could not yet accept this preposterous thought in its entirety, but certainly it would explain a great deal if it were true. It would even explain—I realized suddenly—that strange blanking out in the plane over the Sumatra jungle, that moment from which everything had seemed so wrong.

Perhaps that was the moment when Edward Bond left Earth, and Ganelon took his place—both twins too stunned and helpless at the change to know what had happened, or to understand.

But this was impossible!

"I don't remember!" I said harshly. "It can't have happened. I *know* who I am! I know everything that ever happened to Edward Bond. You can't tell me that all that is only illusion. It's too clear, too real!"

"Ganelon, Ganelon," Edeyrn crooned to me, a smile in her voice. "Think of the rebel tribes. Try, Ganelon. Try to remember why they did what they did to you. The woodrunners, Ganelon— the disobedient little men in green. The hateful men who threatened us. Ganelon, surely you remember!"

It may have been a form of hypnotism. I thought of that later. But at that moment, a picture did swim into my mind. I could see the green-clad swarms moving through the woods, and the sight of them made me hot with sudden anger. For that instant I was Ganelon, and a great and powerful lord, defied by these underlings not fit to tie my shoe.

"Of course you hated them," murmured Edeyrn. She may have seen the look on my face. I felt the stiffness of an unfamiliar twist of feature as she spoke. I had straightened where I sat, and my shoulders had gone back arrogantly, my lip curling a feeling of scorn. So perhaps she did not read my mind at all. What I thought was plain in my face and bearing.

"Of course you punished them when you could," she went on. "It was your right and duty. But they duped you, Ganelon. They were cleverer than you. They found a door that would turn on a temporal axis and thrust you into another world. On the far side of the door was Edward Bond who did not hate them. So they opened the door."

Edeyrn's voice rose slightly and in it I detected a note of mockery.

"False memories, false memories, Ganelon. You put on Edward Bond's past when you put on his identity. But he came into our world as he was, free of any knowledge of Ganelon. He has given us much trouble, my friend, and much bewilderment. At first we did not guess what had gone wrong. It seemed to us that as Ganelon vanished from our Coven, a strange new Ganelon appeared among the rebels, organizing them to fight against his own people." She laughed softly. "We had to rouse Ghast Rhymi from his sleep to aid us. But in the end, learning the method of door- opening, we came to Earth and searched for you, and found you. And brought you back. This is your world, Lord Ganelon! Will you accept it?"

I shook my head dizzily.

"It isn't real. I'm still Edward Bond."

"We can bring back your true memories. And we will. They came to the surface for a moment, I think, just now. But it will take time. Meanwhile, you are one of the Coven, and Edward Bond is back upon Earth in his old place. Remembering—" She laughed softly. "Remembering, I am sure, all he left undone here. But helpless to return, or meddle again in what does not concern him. But we have needed you, Ganelon. How badly we have needed you!"

"What can I do? I'm Edward Bond."

"Ganelon can do much—when he remembers. The Coven has fallen upon evil days. Once we were thirteen. Once there were other Covens to join us in our Sabbats. Once we ruled this whole world, under Great Llyr. But Llyr is falling asleep now. He draws farther and farther away from his worshipers. By degrees the Dark World has fallen into savagery. And, of all the Covens, only we remain, a broken circle, dwelling close to Caer Llyr where the Great One sleeps, beyond his Golden Window."

She fell silent for a moment.

"Sometimes I think that Llyr does not sleep at all," she said. "I think he is withdrawing, little by little, into some farther world, losing his interest in us whom he created. But he returns!" she laughed. "Yes, he returns when the sacrifices stand before his Window. And so long as he comes back, the Coven has power to force its will upon the Dark World.

"But day by day the forest rebels grow stronger, Ganelon. With our help, you were gathering power to oppose them—when you vanished. We needed you then, and we need you more than ever now. You are one of the Coven, perhaps the greatest of us all. With Matholch you were—"

"Wait a minute," I said. "I'm still confused. Matholch? Was he the wolf I saw?"

"He was."

"You spoke of him as though he were a man."

"He *is* a man—at times. He is lycanthropic. A shape-changer."

"A werewolf? That's impossible. It's a myth, a bit of crazy folklore."

"What started the myth?" Edeyrn asked. "Long ago, there were many gateways opened between the Dark World and Earth. On Earth, memories of those days survive as superstitious tales. Folklore. But with roots in reality."

"It's superstition, nothing else," I said flatly. "You actually mean that werewolves, vampires and all that, exist."

"Ghast Rhymi could tell you more of this than I can. But we cannot wake him for such a matter. Perhaps I—well, listen. The body is composed of cells. These are adaptable to some extent. When they are made even more adaptable, when metabolism is accelerated sporadically, werewolves come into being."

The sweet, sexless child's voice spoke on from the shadow of the hood. I began to understand a little. On Earth, college biology had showed me instances of cells run wild—malignant tumors and the like. And there were many cases of "wolf-men," with thick hair growing like a pelt over them. If the cells could adapt themselves *quickly*, strange things might occur.

But the bones? Specialized osseous tissue, not the rigidly brittle bones of the normal man. A physiological structure that could, theoretically, so alter itself that it would be wolf instead of man, was an astounding theory!

"Part of it is illusion, of course," Edeyrn said. "Matholch is not as bestial in form as he seems. Yet he is a shape-changer, and his form does alter."

"But how?" I asked. "How did he get this power?"

For the first time Edeyrn seemed to hesitate. "He is—a mutation. There are many mutations among us, here in the Dark World. Some are in the Coven, but others are elsewhere."

"Are you a mutation?" I asked her.

"Yes."

"A—shape-changer?"

"No," Edeyrn said, and the thin body under the robe seemed to shake a little. "No, I cannot change my shape, Lord Ganelon. You do not remember my—my powers?"

"I do not."

"Yet you may find them useful when the Rebels strike again," she said slowly. "Yes, there are mutations among us, and perhaps that is the chief reason why the probability-rift came ages ago. There are no mutants on Earth—at least not of our type. Matholch is not the only one."

"Am I a mutant?" I asked very softly.

The cowled head shook.

"No. For no mutant may be sealed to Llyr. As you have been sealed. One of the Coven must know the key to Caer Llyr."

The cold breath of fear touched me again. No, not fear. Horror, the deadly, monstrous breathlessness that always took me when the name of Llyr was mentioned.

I forced myself to say, "Who is Llyr?"

There was a long silence.

"Who speaks of Llyr?" a deep voice behind me asked. "Better not to lift *that* veil, Edeyrn!"

"Yet it may be necessary," Edeyrn said.

I turned, and saw, framed against the dark portiere, the rangy, whipcord figure of a man, clad as I was in tunic and trunks. His red, pointed beard jutted; the half-snarling curve of his full lips reminded me of something. Agile grace was in every line of his wiry body.

Yellow eyes watched me with wry amusement.

"Pray it may not be necessary," the man said. "Well, Lord Ganelon? Have you forgotten me, too?"

"He has forgotten you, Matholch," Edeyrn said. "At least in this form!"

Matholch—the wolf! The shape-changer!

He grinned.

"It is Sabbat tonight," he said. "The Lord Ganelon must be prepared for it. Also, I think there will be trouble. However, that is Medea's business, and she asks if Ganelon is awake. Since he is, let us see her now."

"Will you go with Matholch?" Edeyrn asked me.

"I suppose so," I said. The red-beard grinned again.

"Ai, you *have* forgotten, Ganelon! In the old days you'd never have trusted me behind your back with a dagger."

"You always knew better than to strike," Edeyrn said. "If Ganelon ever called on Llyr, it would be unfortunate for you!"

"Well, I joked," Matholch said carelessly. "My enemies must be strong enough to give me a fight so I'll wait till your memory comes back, Lord Ganelon. Meanwhile the Coven has its back to the wall, and I need you as badly as you need me. Will you come?"

"Go with him," Edeyrn said. "You are in no danger—wolf's bark is worse than wolf's bite—even though this is not Caer Llyr."

I thought I sensed a hidden threat in her words. Matholch shrugged and held the curtain aside to let me pass.

"Few dare to threaten a shape-changer," he said over his shoulder.

"I dare," Edeyrn said, from the enigmatic shadows of her saffron cowl. And I remembered she was a mutant too—though not a lycanthrope, like a red-bearded werewolf striding beside me along the vaulted passage.

What was—Edeyrn?

Up to now the true wonder of the situation had not really touched me yet. The anesthesia of shock had dulled me. As a soldier—caught in the white light of a flare dropped from an overhead plane—freezes into immobility, so my mind still remained passive. Only superficial thoughts were moving there, as though, by concentration on immediate needs, I could eliminate the incredible fact that I was not on the familiar, solid ground of Earth.

But it was more than this. There was a curious, indefinable familiarity about these groined, pale-walled halls through which I strode beside Matholch, as there had been a queer familiarity about the twilit landscape stretching to forested distance beneath the window of my room.

Edeyrn—Medea—the Coven.

The names had significance, like words in a language I had once known well, but had forgotten.

The half-loping, swift walk of Matholch, the easy swing of his muscular shoulders, the snarling smile on his red-bearded lips—these were not new to me.

He watched me furtively out of his yellow eyes. Once we paused before a red-figured drapery, and Matholch, hesitating, thrust the curtain aside and gestured me forward.

I took one step—and stopped. I looked at him.

He nodded as though satisfied. Yet there was still a question in his face.

"So you remember a little, eh? Enough to know that this isn't the way to Medea. However, come along, for a moment. I want to talk to you."

As I followed him up a winding stair, I suddenly realized that he had not spoken in English. But I had understood him, as I had understood Edeyrn and Medea.

Ganelon?

We were in a tower room, walled with transparent panes. There was a smoky, sour odor in the air, and gray tendrils coiled up from a brazier set in a tripod in the middle of the chamber. Matholch gestured me to one of the couches by the windows. He dropped carelessly beside me.

"I wonder how much you remember," he said.

I shook my head.

"Not much. Enough not to be too—trusting."

"The artificial Earth-memories are still strong, then. Ghast Rhymi said you would remember eventually, but that it would take time. The false writing on the slate of your mind will fade, and the old, true memories will come back. After a while."

Like a palimpsest, I thought—manuscript with two writings upon its parchment. But Ganelon was still a stranger; I was still Edward Bond.

"I wonder," Matholch said slowly, staring at me. "You spent much time exiled. I wonder if you have changed, basically. Always before—you hated me, Ganelon. Do you hate me now?"

"No," I said. "At least, I don't know. I think I distrust you."

"You have reason. If you remember at all. We have always been enemies, Ganelon, though bound together by the needs and laws of the Coven. I wonder if we need be enemies any longer?"

"It depends. I'm not anxious to make enemies—especially here."

Matholch's red brows drew together.

"Ai, that is not Ganelon speaking! In the old days, you cared nothing about how many enemies you made. If you have changed so much, danger to us all may result."

"My memory is gone," I said. "I don't understand much of this. It seems dream-like."

Now he sprang up and restlessly paced the room. "That's well. If you become the old Ganelon again, we'll be enemies again. That I know. But if Earth-exile has changed you—altered you— we may be friends. It would be better to be friends. Medea would not like it; I do not think Edeyrn would. As for Ghast Rhymi—" He shrugged. "Ghast Rhymi is old—old. In all the Dark World, Ganelon, you have the most power. Or can have. But it would mean going to Caer Llyr."

Matholch stooped to look into my eyes.

"In the old days, you knew what that meant. You were afraid, but you wanted the power. Once you went to Caer Llyr—to be sealed. So there is a bond between you and Llyr—not consummated yet. But it can be, if you wish it."

"What is Llyr?" I asked.

"Pray that you will not remember that," Matholch said. "When Medea talks to you—beware when she speaks of Llyr. I may be friend of yours or enemy, Ganelon, but for my own sake, for the sake of the Dark World—even for the sake of the rebels—I warn you: do not go to Caer Llyr. No matter what Medea asks. Or promises. At least be wary till you have your memories back."

"What is Llyr?" I asked again.

Matholch swung around, his back to me. "Ghast Rhymi knows, I think. I do not. Nor do I want to. Llyr is—is evil—and is hungry, always. But what feeds his appetite is—is—"He stopped.

"You have forgotten," he went on after a while. "One thing I wonder. Have you forgotten how to summon Llyr?"

I did not answer. There was a darkness in my mind, an ebon gate against which my questioning thoughts probed vainly.

Llyr—Llyr?

Matholch cast a handful of powdery substance into the glowing brazier.

"Can you summon Llyr?" he asked again his voice soft. "Answer, Ganelon. Can you?"

The sour smoke-stench grew stronger. The darkness in my head sprang apart, riven, as though a gateway had opened in the shadow. I—recognized that deadly perfume.

I stood up, glaring at Matholch. I took two steps, thrust out my sandaled foot and overturned the brazier. Embers scattered on the stone floor. The red-beard turned a startled face to me.

I reached out, gripped Matholch's tunic, and shook him till his teeth rattled together. Hot fury filled me—and something more.

That Matholch should try his tricks on me!

A stranger had my tongue. I heard myself speaking.

"Save your spells for the slaves and helots," I snarled. "I tell you what I wish to tell you—no more than that! Burn your filthy herbs elsewhere, not in my presence!"

Red-bearded jaw jutted. Yellow eyes flamed. Matholch's face altered, flesh flowing like water, dimly seen in the smoke-clouds that poured up from the scattered embers.

Yellow tusks threatened me through the gray mists.

The shape-changer made a wordless noise in his throat—the guttural sound a beast might make. Wolf-cry! A wolf mask glared into mine!

The smoke swam away. The illusion—illusions?—was gone. Matholch, his face relaxing from its snarling lines, pulled gently free from my grip.

"You—startled me, Lord Ganelon," he said smoothly. "But I think that I have had a question answered, whether or not these herbs—" He nodded toward the overturned brazier. "—had anything to do with it."

I turned toward the doorway.

"Wait," Matholch said. "I took something from you, a while ago."

I stopped.

The red-beard came toward me, holding out a weapon—a bared sword.

"I took this from you when we passed through the Need-fire," he said. "It is yours."

I accepted the blade.

Again I moved toward the curtained archway.

Behind me Matholch spoke.

"We are not enemies yet, Ganelon," he said gently. "And, if you are wise, you will not forget my warning. Do not go to Caer Llyr."

I went out. Holding the sword, I hurried down the winding stairway. My feet found their path without conscious guidance. The—intruder—in my brain was still strong. A palimpsest. And the blurred, erased writing was becoming visible, as though treated with some strong chemical.

The writing that was my lost memory.

The castle—how did I know it was a castle?—was a labyrinth. Twice I passed silent soldiers standing guard, with a familiar shadow of fear in their eyes—a shadow that, I thought, deepened as they saw me.

I went on, hurrying along a pale-amber hallway. I brushed aside a golden curtain and stepped into an oval room, dome-ceilinged, walled with pale, silken draperies. A fountain spurted, its spray cool on my cheek. Across the chamber, an archway showed the outlines of leafy branches beyond.

I went through the arch. I stepped out into a walled garden. A garden of exotic flowers and bizarre trees.

The blooms were a riot of patternless color, like glowing jewels against the dark earth. Ruby and amethyst, crystal-clear and milky white, silver and gold and emerald, the flowers made a motionless carpet. But the trees were not motionless.

Twisted and gnarled as oaks, their black boles and branches were veiled by a luxuriant cloud of leafage, virulent green.

A stir of movement rippled through that green curtain. The trees roused to awareness.

I saw the black branches twist and writhe slowly—

Satisfied, their vigilance relaxed. They were motionless again. They—knew me.

Beyond that evil orchard the dark sky made the glowing ember of the sun more brilliant by contrast.

The trees stirred again.

Ripples of unrest shook the green. A serpentine limb, training a veil of leaves, lashed out—struck—whipped back into place.

Where it had been a darting shape ran forward, ducking and twisting as the guardian trees struck savagely at it.

A man, in a tight-fitting suit of earth-brown and forest green, came running toward me, his feet trampling the jewel-flowers. His hard, reckless face was alight with excitement and a kind of triumph. He was empty-handed, but a pistol-like weapon of some sort swung at his belt.

"Edward!" he said urgently, yet keeping his voice low, "Edward Bond!"

I knew him. Or I knew him for what he was. I had seen dodging, furtive, green-clad figures like this before, and an anger already familiar surged over me at the very sight of him.

Enemy, upstart! One of the many who had dared work their magic upon the great Lord Ganelon.

I felt the heat of rage suffuse my face, and the blood rang in my ears with this unfamiliar, yet well-known fury. My body stiffened in the posture of Ganelon—shoulders back, lip curled, chin high. I heard myself curse the fellow in a voice that was choked and a language I scarcely remembered.

And I saw him draw back, disbelief vivid upon his face. His hand dropped to his belt.

"Ganelon?" he faltered, his eyes narrow as they searched mine. "Edward, are you with us or are you Ganelon again?"

Gripped in my right hand I still held the sword. I cut at him savagely by way of answer. He sprang back, glanced over his shoulder, and drew his weapon. I followed his glance and saw another green figure dodging forward among the trees. It was smaller and slenderer—a girl, in a tunic the color of earth and forest. Her black hair swung upon her shoulders. She was tugging at her belt as she ran, and the face she turned to me was ugly with hate, her teeth showing in a snarl.

The man before me was saying something.

"Edward, listen to me!" he was crying. "Even if you're Ganelon, you remember Edward Bond! He was with us—he believed in us. Give us a hearing before it's too late! Arles could convince you, Edward! Come to Arles. Even if you're Ganelon, let me take you to Arles!"

"It's no use, Ertu," the voice of the girl cried thinly. She was struggling with the last of the trees, whose flexible bough-tips still clutched to stop her. Neither of them tried now to keep their voices down. They were shouting, and I knew they must rouse the guards at any moment, and I wanted to kill them both myself before anyone came to forestall me by accident. I was hungry and thirsty for the blood of these enemies, and in that moment the name of Edward Bond was not even memory.

"Kill him, Ertu!" cried the girl. "Kill him or stand out of the way! I know Ganelon!"

I looked at her and took a fresh grip on my sword. Yes, she spoke the truth. She knew Ganelon. And Ganelon knew her, and remembered dimly that she had reason for her hate. I had seen that face before, contorted with fury and despair. I could not recall when or where or why, but she looked familiar.

The man Ertu drew his weapon reluctantly. To him I was still at least the image of a friend. I laughed exultantly and swung at him again with the sword, hearing it hiss viciously through the air. This time I drew blood. He stepped back again, lifting his weapon so that I looked down its black barrel.

"Don't make me do it," he said between his teeth. "This will pass. You have been Edward Bond—you will be again. Don't make me kill you, Ganelon!"

I lifted the sword, seeing him only dimly through a ruddy haze of anger. There was a great exultation in me. I could already see the fountain of blood that would leap from his severed arteries when my blade completed its swing.

I braced my body for a great full-armed blow!

And the sword came alive in my hand. It leaped and shuddered against my fist.

Impossibly—in a way I cannot describe—that blow reversed itself. All the energy I was braced to expend upon my enemy recoiled up the sword, up my arm, crashed against my own body. A violent explosion of pain and shock sent the garden reeling. The earth struck hard against my knees.

Mist cleared from my eyes. I was still Ganelon, but a Ganelon dizzy from something more powerful than a blow.

I was kneeling on the grass, braced with one hand, shaking the throbbing fingers of my sword-hand and staring at the sword that lay a dozen feet away, still faintly glowing.

It was Matholch's doing—I knew that! I should have remembered how little I could trust that shifting, unstable wolfing. I had laid hands upon him in his tower-room—I should have known he would have his revenge for that. Even Edward Bond—soft fool that he was—would have been wise enough not to accept a gift from the shape-changer.

There was no time now for anger at Matholch, though. I was looking up into Ertu's eyes, and into the muzzle of his weapon, and the look of decision grew slowly in his face as he scanned mine.

"Ganelon!" he said, almost whispering, "Warlock!"

He titled the weapon down at me, his finger moving on the trigger.

"Wait, Ertu!" cried a thin voice behind him. "Wait—let me!"

I looked up, still dazed. It had all happened so quickly that the girl was still struggling in the edge of the trees, though she cleared them as I looked and lifted her own weapon. Behind it her face was white and blazing with relentless hate. "Let me!" she cried again. "He owed me this!"

I was helpless. I knew that even at this distance she would not miss. I saw the glare of fury in her eyes and I saw the muzzle waver a little as her hand shook with rage, but I knew she would not miss me. I thought of a great many things in that instant— confused memories of Ganelon's and of Edward Bond's surged together through my mind.

Then a great hissing like a wind swept up among the trees behind the girl. They all swayed toward her more swiftly than trees have any right to move, stooping and straining and hissing with a dreadful vicious avidity. Ertu shouted something inarticulate. But I think the girl was too angry to hear or see.

She never knew what happened. She could only have felt the great bone-cracking sweep of the nearest branch, reaching out for her from the leaning tree. She fired as the blow struck her, and a white-hot bolt ploughed up the turf at my knee. I could smell the charring grass.

The girl screamed thinly once as the avid boughs writhed together over her. The limbs threshed about her in a furious welter, and I heard one clear and distinct snap—a sound I had heard before, I knew, in this garden. The human spine is no more than a twig in the grip of those mighty boughs.

Ertu was stunned for one brief instant. Then he whirled to me, and this time I knew his finger would not hesitate on the trigger.

But time had run out for the two woodspeople. He was not fully turned when there came a laugh, cool and amused, from behind me. I saw loathing and hatred flash across Ertu's bronzed face, and the weapon whirled away from me and pointed toward someone at my back. But before he could press the trigger something like an arrow of white light sprang over my shoulder and stuck him above the heart.

He dropped instantly, his mouth frozen in a snarling square, his eyes staring.

I turned, getting slowly to my feet. Medea stood there smiling, very slim and lovely in a close-fitting scarlet gown. In her hand was a small black rod, still raised. Her purple eyes met mine.

"Ganelon," she murmured in an infinitely caressing voice. "Ganelon." And still holding my gaze with hers, she clapped her hands softly.

Silent, swift-moving guardsmen came and lifted the motionless body of Ertu. They carried him away. The trees stirred, whispered—and fell silent.

"You have remembered," Medea said. "Ganelon is ours again. Do you remember me—Lord Ganelon?"

Medea, witch of Colchis! Black and white and crimson, she stood there smiling at me, her strange loveliness stirring old, forgotten memories in my blood. No man who had known Medea could ever forget her wholly. Not till time ended. ·

But wait! There was something more about Medea that I must remember. Something that made even Ganelon a little doubtful, a little cautious. Ganelon? Was I Ganelon again? I had been wholly my old self when the woodspeople stood before me, but now I was uncertain.

The memories ebbed. While the lovely witch stood smiling at me, not guessing, all that had made me so briefly Ganelon dropped from my mind and body like a discarded cloak. Edward Bond stood there in my clothing, staring about the clearing and remembering with dismay and sick revulsion what had just been happening here.

For a moment I turned away to hide from Medea what my face must betray if she saw it. I felt dizzy with more than memory. The knowledge that two identities shared my body was a thought even more disturbing than the memory of what I had just done in the grip of Ganelon's strong, evil will.

This was Ganelon's body. There could be no doubt of it now. Somewhere on Earth Edward Bond was back in his old place, but the patterns of his memory still overlaid my mind, so that he and I shared a common soul, and there was no Ganelon except briefly, in snatches, as the memories that were rightfully mine— mine?—returned to crowd out Edward Bond.

I hated Ganelon. I rejected all he thought and was. My false memories, the heritage from Edward Bond, were stronger in me than Ganelon. I was Edward Bond—now!

Medea's caressing voice broke in upon my conflict, echoing her question.

"Do you remember me, Lord Ganelon?"

I turned to her, feeling the bewilderment on my own face, so that my very thoughts were blurred.

"My name is Bond," I told her stubbornly.

She sighed.

"You will come back," she said. "It will take time, but Ganelon will return to us. As you see familiar things again, the life of the Dark World, the life of the Coven, the doors of your mind will open once more. You will remember a little more tonight, I think, at the Sabbat." Her red smile was suddenly almost frightening.

"Not since I went into the Earth-world has a Sabbat been held, and it is long past time," she went on. "For in Caer Llyr there is one who stirs and grows hungry for his sacrifice."

She looked at me piercingly, the purple eyes narrowing.

"Do you remember Caer Llyr, Ganelon?"

The old sickness and horror came over me as she repeated that cryptic name.

Llyr—Llyr! Darkness, and something stirring beyond a golden window. Something too alien to touch the soil that human feet touched, something that should never share the same life humans lived. Touching that soil, sharing that life, it defiled them so that they were no longer fit for humans to share. And yet, despite my revulsion, Llyr was terribly intimate, too!

I knew, I remembered—

"I remember nothing," I told her shortly. For in that particular moment, caution was born in me. I could not trust anyone, not even myself. Least of all Ganelon—myself. I *did* remember, but I must not let them know. Until I was clearer as to what they wanted, what they threatened, I must keep this one secret which was all the weapon I had.

Llyr! The thought of him—of it—crystallized that decision in my mind. For somewhere in the murk of Ganelon's past there was a frightening link with Llyr. I knew they were trying to push me into that abyss of oneness with Llyr, and I sensed that even Ganelon feared that. I must pretend to be more ignorant than I really was until the thing grew clearer in my memory.

I shook my head again. "I remembered nothing."

"Not even Medea?" she whispered, and swayed toward me. There was sorcery about her. My arms received that red and white softness as if they were Ganelon's arms, not mine. But it was Edward Bond's lips which responded to the fierce pressure of her lips.

Not even Medea?

Edward Bond or Ganelon, what was it to me then? The moment the enough.

But the touch of the red witch wrought a change in Edward Bond. It brought a sense of strangeness, of utter strangeness, to him—to me. I held her lovely, yielding body in my arms, but something alien and unknown stooped and hovered above me as we touched. I surmised that she was holding herself in check— restraining a—a demon that possessed her—a demon that fought to free itself.

"Ganelon!"

Trembling, she pressed her palms against my chest and thrust free. Tiny droplets stood on her pale forehead.

"Enough!" she whispered. "You know!"

"What, Medea?"

And now stark horror stood in those purple eyes.

"You have forgotten!" she said. "You have forgotten me, forgotten who I am, *what* I am!"

Later, in the apartments that had been Ganelon's, I waited for the hour of Sabbat. And as I waited, I paced the floor restlessly. Ganelon's feet, pacing Ganelon's floor. But the man who walked here was Edward Bond. Amazing, I thought, how the false memory-patterns of another person, impressed upon Ganelon's clean-sponged brain, had changed him from himself to—me.

I wonder if I would ever be sure again which personality was myself. I hated and distrusted Ganelon, now. But I knew how easily the old self slipped back, in which I would despise Edward Bond.

And yet to save myself, I must call back Ganelon's memories. I must know more than those around me guessed I knew, or I thought Ganelon and Bond together might be lost. Medea would tell me nothing. Edeyrn would tell me nothing. Matholch might tell me much, but he would be lying.

I scarcely dared go with them to this Sabbat, which I thought would be the Sabbat of Llyr, because of that strange and terrible link between Llyr and myself. There would be sacrifices.

How could I be sure I, myself, was not destined for the altar before that—that golden window?

Then, for a brief but timeless moment Ganelon came back, re-membering fragmentary things that flitted through my mind too swiftly to take shape. I caught only terror—terror and revulsion and a hideous, hopeless longing . . ..

Dared I attend the Sabbat?

But I dared not fail to attend, for if I refused I must admit I knew more about what threatened Ganelon than Edward Bond should know. And my only frail weapon against them now was what little I recalled that was secret from them. I must go. Even if the altar waited me, I must go.

There were the woodspeople. They were outlaws, hunted through the forests by Coven soldiers. Capture meant enslavement—I remembered the look of still horror in the eyes of those living dead men who were Medea's servants. As Edward Bond, I pitied them, wondered if I could do anything to save them from the coven. The real Edward Bond had been living among them for a year and a half, organizing resistance, fighting the Coven. On Earth, I knew, he must be raging helplessly now, haunted by the knowledge of work unfinished and friends abandoned to the mercies of dark magic.

Perhaps I should seek the woodspeople out. Among them, at least, I would be safe while my memories returned. But when they returned—why, then Ganelon would rage, running amuck among them, mad with his own fury and arrogance. Dared I subject the woodspeople to the danger that would be the Lord Ganelon when Ganelon's memories came back? Dared I subject myself to their vengeance, for they would be many against one?

I could not go and I could not stay. There was safety nowhere for the Edward Bond who might become Ganelon at any moment. There was danger everywhere. From the rebel woodspeople, from every member of this Coven.

It might come through the wild and mocking Matholch.

Or through Edeyrn, who had watched me unseen with her chilling gaze in the shadows of her cowl.

Through Ghast Rhymi, whoever *he* was. Through Arles, or through the red witch!

Yes, most of all, I thought, through Medea—Medea, whom I loved!

At dusk, two maidens—helot-servants—came, bringing food and a change of garments. I ate hurriedly, dressed in the plain, fine-textured tunic and shorts, and drew about me the royal blue cloak they had carried. A mask of golden cloth I dangled undecidedly, until one of the maidens spoke:

"We are to guide you when you are ready, Lord," she reminded me.

"I'm ready now," I said, and followed the pair.

A pale, concealed lighting system of some sort made the hallways bright. I was taken to Medea's apartment, with its singing fountain under the high dome. The red witch was there breathtakingly lovely in a clinging robe of pure white. Above the robe her naked shoulders gleamed smoothly. She wore a scarlet cloak. I wore a blue one.

The helots slipped away. Medea smiled at me, but I noticed a wire-taut tenseness about her, betrayingly visible at the corners of her lips and in her eyes. A pulse of expectation seemed to beat out from her.

"Are you ready, Ganelon?"

"I don't know," I said. "It depends, I suppose. Don't forget that my memory's gone."

"It may return tonight, some of it anyway," she said. "But you will take no part in the ritual, at least until after the sacrifice. It will be better if you merely watch. Since you do not remember the rites, you'd best leave those to the rest of the Coven."

"Matholch?"

"And Edeyrn," Medea said. "Ghast Rhymi will not come. He never leaves this castle, nor will he unless the need is very great. He is old, too old."

I frowned at the red witch. "Where are we going?" I asked.

"To Caer Sécaire. I told you there has been no sacrifice since I went to Earth-world to search for you. It is past time."

"What am I supposed to do?"

She put out a slender hand and touched mine.

"Nothing, till the moment comes. You will know then. But meantime you must watch—no more than that. Put on your mask now."

She slipped on a small black mask that left the lower half of her face visible.

I donned the golden mask. I followed Medea to a curtained archway, and through it.

We were in a courtyard. Two horses stood waiting, held by grooms. Medea mounted one and I the other.

Overhead the sky had darkened. A huge door lifted in the wall. Beyond, a roadway stretched toward the distant forest.

The somber, angry disc of the red sun, swollen and burning with a dull fire, touched the crest of the mountain barrier.

Swiftly it sank. Darkness came across the sky with a swooping rush. A million points of white light became visible. In the faint starshine Medea's face was ghost-pale.

Through the near-darkness her eyes glowed.

Faintly, and from far away, I heard a thin, trumpeting call. It was repeated.

Then silence—and a whispering that rose to a rhythmic thudding of shod hoofs.

Past us moved a figure, a helot guardsman, unmasked, un-speaking, his gaze turned to the waiting gateway.

Then another—and another. Until three score of soldiers had gone past, and after them nearly three score of maidens—the slave-girls.

On a light, swift-looking roan stallion Matholch came by, stealing a glance at me from his yellow eyes. A cloak of forest green swirled from his shoulders.

Behind him, the tiny form of Edeyrn, on a pony suited to her smallness. She was still cowled, her face hidden, but she now wore a cloak of purest yellow.

Medea nodded at me. We touched our heels to the horses' flanks and took our places in the column. Behind us other figures rode, but I could not see them clearly. It was too dark.

Through the gateway in the wall we went, still in silence save for the clopping of hoofs. We rode across the plain. The edges of the forest reached out toward us and swallowed us.

I glanced behind. An enormous bulk against the sky showed the castle I had left.

We rode under heavy, drooping branches. These were not the black trees of Medea's garden, but they were not normal either. I could not tell why an indefinable sense of strangeness reached out at me from the dim shadows above and around us.

After a long time the ground dipped at our feet, and we saw below us the road's end. The moon had risen belatedly. By its yellow glare there materialized from the deep valley below us a sort of tower, a dark, windowless structure almost Gothic in plan, as though it had thrust itself from the black earth, from the dark grove of ancient and alien trees.

Caer Sécaire!

I had been here before. Ganelon of the Dark World knew this spot well. But I did not know it; I sensed only that unpleasant familiarity, the *déjà vu* phenomenon, known to all psychologists, coupled with a curious depersonalization, as though my own body, my mind, my very soul, felt altered and strange.

Caer Sécaire. Sécaire? Somewhere, in my studies, I had encountered that name. An ancient rite, in—in Gascony, that was it!

The Mass of Saint Sécaire!

And the man for whom that Black Mass is said—dies. That, too, I remembered. Was the Mass to be said for Ganelon tonight?

This was not the Place of Llyr. Somehow I knew that. Caer Llyr was elsewhere and otherwise, not a temple, not a place visited by worshipers. But here in Caer Sécaire, as in other temples throughout the Dark Land, Llyr might be summoned to his feasting, and, summoned, would come.

Would Ganelon be his feast tonight? I clenched the reins with nervous hands. There was some tension in the air that I could not quite understand. Medea was calm beside me. Edeyrn was always calm. Matholch, I could swear, had nothing to take the place of nerves. Yet in the night there was tension, as if it breathed upon us from the dark trees along the roadside.

Before us, in a silent, submissive flock, the soldiers and the slave-girls went. Some of the soldiers were armed. They seemed to be herding the rest, their movements mechanical, as if whatever had once made them free-willed humans was now asleep. I knew without being told the purpose for which those men and maidens were being driven toward Caer Sécaire. But not even these voiceless mindless victims were tense. They went blindly to their doom. No, the tension came from the dark around us.

Someone, something, waiting in the night!

From out of the dark woods, suddenly, startlingly, a trumpet-note rang upon the air. In the same instant there was a wild crashing in the underbrush, an outburst of shouts and cries, and the night was laced by the thin lightnings of unfamiliar gunfire. The road was suddenly thronging with green-clad figures who swarmed about the column of slaves ahead of us, grappling with the guards, closing in between us and the mindless victims at our forefront.

My horse reared wildly. I fought him hard, forcing him down again, while stirrings of the old red rage I had felt before mounted in my brain. Ganelon, at sight of the forest people, struggled to take control. Him too I fought. Even in my surprise and bewilderment, I saw in this interruption the possibility of succor. I cracked my rearing horse between the ears with clubbed rein-loops and struggled to keep my balance.

Beside me Medea had risen in her stirrups and was sending bolt after arrowy bold into the green melee ahead of us, the dark rod that was her weapon leaping in her hand with every shot. Edeyrn had drawn aside, taking no part in the fight. Her small cowled figure sat crouching in the saddle, but her very stillness was alarming. I had the feeling she could end the combat in a moment if she chose.

As for Matholch, his saddle was empty. His horse was already crashing away through the woods, and Matholch had hurled himself headlong into the fight, snarling joyously. The sound sent cold shudders down my spine. I could see that his green cloak covered a shape that was not wholly manlike, and the green people veered away from him as he plunged through their throngs toward the head of the column.

The woodsfolk were trying a desperate rescue. I realized that immediately. I saw too that they dared not attack the Coven itself. All their efforts were aimed at over-powering the robotlike guards so that the equally robotlike victims might be saved from Llyr. And I could see that they were failing.

For the victims were too apathetic to scatter. All will had long ago been drained away from them. They obeyed orders—that was all. And the forest people were leaderless. In a moment or two I realized that, and knew why. It was my fault. Edward Bond may have planned this daring raid, but through my doing, he was not here to guide them. And already the abortive fight was nearly over.

Medea's flying fiery arrows struck down man after man. The mindless guards fired stolidly into the swarms that surged about them, and Matholch's deep-throated, exultant, snarling yells as he fought his way toward his soldiers were more potent than weapons. The raiders shrank back from the sound as they did not shrink from gunfire. In a moment, I knew, Matholch would reach his men, and organized resistance would break the back of this unguided mutiny.

For an instant my own mind was a fierce battle-ground. Ganelon struggled to take control, and Edward Bond resisted him savagely.

As Ganelon I knew my place was beside the wolfling; every instinct urged me forward to his side. But Edward Bond knew better. Edward Bond too knew where his rightful place should be.

I shoved up my golden mask so that my face was visible. I drove my heels into my horse's sides and urged him headlong down the road behind Matholch. The sheer weight of the horse gave me an advantage Matholch, afoot, did not have. The sound of drumming hoofs and the lunging shoulders of my mount opened a way for me. I rose in the stirrups and shouted with Ganelon's deep, carrying roar:

"Bond! Bond! Edward Bond!"

The rebels heard me. For an instant the battle around the column wavered as every green-clad man paused to look back. Then they saw their lost leader, and a great echoing hail swept their ranks.

"Bond! Edward Bond!"

The forest rang with it, and there was new courage in the sound. Matholch's wild snarl of rage was drowned in the roar of the forest men as they surged forward again to the attack.

Out of Ganelon's memories I knew what I must do. The foresters were dragging down guard after guard, careless of the gunfire that mowed their disordered ranks. But only I could save the prisoners. Only Ganelon's voice could pierce the daze that held them.

I kicked my frantic horse forward, knocking guards left and right, and gained the head of the column.

"In the forest!" I shouted. "Waken and run! Run hard!"

There was an instant forward surge as the slaves, still tranced in their dreadful dream, but obedient to the voice of a Coven member, lurched through the thin rank of their guard. The whole shape of the struggle changed as the core of it streamed irresistibly forward across the road and into the darkness of the woods.

The green-clad attackers fell back to let the slaves through. It was strange, voiceless flight they made. Not even the guards shouted, through they fired and fired again upon the retreating column, their faces as blank as if they slept without dreams.

My flesh crawled as I watched that sight—the men and women fleeing for their lives, the armed soldiers shooting them down, and the faces of them all utterly without expression. Voiceless they ran and voiceless they died when the gun-bolts found them.

I wrenched my horse around and kicked him in the wake of the fleeing column. My golden mask slipped sidewise and I tore it off, waving to the scattering foresters, the moonlight catching brightly on its gold.

"Save yourselves!" I shouted, "Scatter and follow me!"

Behind me I heard Matholch's deep snarl, very near. I glanced over one shoulder as my horse plunged across the road. The shape-changer's tall figure raced me across the heads of several of his soldiers. His face was a wolf-like snarling mask, and as I looked he lifted a dark rod like the one Medea had been using. I saw the arrow of white fire leap from it, and ducked in the saddle.

The movement saved me. I felt a strong tug at my shoulders where the blue cape swirled out, and heard the tear of fabric as the bolt ripped through it and plunged hissing into the dark beyond. My horse lunged on into the woods.

Then the trees were rustling all about me, and my bewildered horse stumbled and tossed up his head, whinnying in terror. Beside me in the dark a soft voice spoke softly.

"This way," it said, and a hand seized the bridle.

I let the woodsmen lead me into the darkness.

It was just dawn when our weary column came to the end of the journey, to the valley between cliffs where the woodsmen had established their stronghold. All of us were tired, though the blank-faced slaves we had rescued trudged on in an irregular column behind me, unaware that their feet were torn and their bodies drooping with exhaustion.

The forest men slipped through the trees around us, alert for followers. We had no wounded with us. The bolts the Coven shot never wounded. Whoever was struck fell dead in their tracks.

In the pale dawn I would not have known the valley before me for the headquarters of a populous clan. It looked quite empty except for scattered boulders, mossy slopes, and a small stream that trickled down the middle, pink in the light of sunrise.

One of the men took my horse then, and we went on foot up the valley, the robot slaves crowding behind. We seemed to be advancing up an empty valley. But when we had gone half its length, suddenly the woodsman at my right laid his hand upon my arm, and we paused, the rabble behind us jostling together without a murmur. Around me the woodsmen laughed softly. I looked up.

She stood high upon a boulder that overhung the stream. She was dressed like a man in a tunic of soft, velvety green, cross-belted with a weapon swinging at each hip, but her hair was a fabulous mantel streaming down over her shoulders and hanging almost to her knees in a cascade of pale gold that rippled like water. A crown of pale gold leaves the color of the hair held it away from her face, and under the shining chaplet she looked down and smiled at us. Especially she smiled at me—at Edward Bond.

And her face was very lovely. It had the strength and innocence and calm serenity of a saint's face, but there was warmth and humor in the red lips. Her eyes were the same color as her tunic, deep green, a color I had never seen before in my own world.

"Welcome back, Edward Bond," she said in a clear, sweet gently hushed voice, as if she had spoken softly for so many years that even now she did not dare speak aloud.

She jumped down from the boulder, very lightly, moving with the sureness of a wild creature that had lived all its lifetime it the woods, as indeed I suppose she had. Her hair floated about her as lightly as a web, settling only slowly about her shoulders as she came forward, so that she seemed to walk in a halo of her own pale gold.

I remembered what the woodsman Ertu had said to me in Medea's garden before her arrow struck him down.

"Arles could convince you, Edward! Even if you're Ganelon, let me take you to Arles!"

I stood before Arles now. Of that I was sure. And if I had needed any conviction before that the woodsmen's cause was mine, this haloed girl would have convinced me with her first words. But as for Ganelon—

How could I know what Ganelon would do?

That question was answered for me. Before my lips could frame worlds, before I could plan my next reaction, Arles came toward me, utterly without pretense or consciousness of the watching eyes. She put her hands on my shoulders and kissed me on the mouth.

And that was not like Medea's kiss—no! Arles' lips were cool and sweet, not warm with the dangerous, alluring honey-musk of the red witch. That intoxication of strange passion I remembered when I had held Medea in my arms did not sweep me now. There was a—a purity about Arles, an honesty that made me suddenly, horribly homesick for Earth.

She drew back. Her moss-green eyes met mine with quiet understanding. She seemed to be waiting.

"Arles," I said, after a moment.

And that seemed to satisfy her. The vague question that had begun to show on her face was gone.

"I wondered," she said. "They didn't hurt you, Edward?"

Instinctively I knew what I had to say.

"No. We hadn't reached Caer Sécaire. If the woodsmen hadn't attacked—well, there'd have been a sacrifice."

Arles reached out and lifted a corner of my torn cloak, her slim fingers light on the silken fabric.

"The blue robe," she said. "Yes, that is the color the sacrifice wears. The gods cast their dice on our side tonight Edward. Now as for this foul thing, we must get rid of it."

Her green eyes blazed. She ripped the cloak from me, tore it across and dropped it to the ground.

"You will not go hunting again alone," she added. "I told you it was dangerous. But you laughed at me. I'll wager you didn't laugh when the Coven slaves caught you! Or was that the way of it?"

I nodded. A slow, deep fury was rising within me. So blue was the color of sacrifice, was it? My fears hadn't been groundless. At Caer Sécaire I would have been the offering, going blindly to my doom. Matholch had known, of course. Trust his wolf-mind to ap-preciate the joke. Edeyrn, thinking her cool, inhuman thoughts in the shadow of her hood, she had known too. And Medea?

Medea!

She had dared betray me! Me, *Ganelon!*

The Opener of the Gate, the Chosen of Llyr, the great Lord Ganelon! They dared! Black thunder roared through my brain. I thought: By Llyr, but they'll suffer for this! They'll crawl to my feet like dogs. Begging my mercy!

Rage had opened the floodgates, and Edward Bond was no more than a set of thin memories that had slipped from me as the blue cloak had slipped from my shoulders—the blue cloak of the chosen sacrifice, on the shoulders of the Lord Ganelon!

I blinked blindly around the green-clad circle. How had I come here? How dared these woodspeoples stand in defiance before me? Blood roared in my ears and the woodland swam around me. When it steadied I would draw my weapon and reap these upstarts as a mower reaps his wheat.

But wait!

First, the Coven, my sworn comrades, had betrayed me. Why, *why?* They had been glad enough to see me when they brought me back from the other world, the alien land of Earth. The woodsmen I could slay whenever I wished it—the other problem came first. And Ganelon was a wise man. I might need these woodspeople to help me in my vengeance. Afterward—ah, afterward!

I strove hard with memory. What could have happened to turn the Coven against me? I could have sworn this had not been Medea's original intention—she had welcomed me back too sincerely for that. Matholch could have influenced her, but again, why, why? Or perhaps it was Edeyrn, or the Old One himself, Ghast Rhymi. In any case, by the Golden Window that opens on the Abyss, they'd learn their error!

"Edward!" a woman's voice, sweet and frightened, came to me as if from a great distance. I fought my way up through a whirlpool of fury and hatred. I saw a pale face haloed in floating hair, the green eyes troubled. I remembered.

Beside Arles stood a stranger, a man whose cold gray eyes upon mine provided the shock I needed to bring me back to sanity. He looked at me as if he knew me—knew Ganelon. I had never seen the man before.

He was short and sturdy, young-looking in spite of the gray flecks in his close-cropped beard. His face was tanned so deeply it had almost the color of the brown earth. In his close-fitting green suit he was the perfect personification of a woodrunner, a glider through the forest, unseen and dangerous. Watching the powerful flex of his muscles when he moved, I knew he would be a bad antagonist. And there was deep antagonism in the way he looked at me.

A white, jagged scar had knotted his right cheek, quirking up his thin mouth so that he wore a perpetual crooked, sardonic half-grin. There was no laughter in those gelid gray eyes, though.

And I saw that the circle of woodsmen had drawn back, ringing us, watching.

The bearded man put out his arm and swept Arles behind him. Unarmed, he stepped forward, toward me.

"No, Lorryn," Arles cried. "Don't hurt him."

Lorryn thrust his face into mine.

"Ganelon!" he said.

And at the name a whisper of fear, of hatred, murmured around the circle of woodsfolk. I saw furtive movements, hands slipping quietly toward the hilts of weapons. I saw Arles' face change.

The old-time cunning of Ganelon came to my aid.

"No," I said, rubbing my forehead. "I'm Bond, all right. It was that drug the Coven gave me. It's still working."

"What drug?"

"I don't know," I told Lorryn. "It was in Medea's wine that I drank. And the long journey tonight has tired me."

I took a few unsteady paces aside and leaned against the boulder, shaking my head as though to clear it. But my ears were alert. The low murmur of suspicion was dying.

Cool fingers touched mine.

"Oh, my dear," Arles said, and whirled on Lorryn. "Do you think I don't know Edward Bond from Ganelon? Lorryn, you're a fool!"

"If the two weren't identical, we'd never have switched them in the first place," Lorryn said roughly. "Be sure, Arles. Very sure!"

Now the whispering grew again. "Better to be sure," the woodsmen murmured. "No risks, Arles! If this is Ganelon, he must die."

The doubt came back into Arles' green eyes. She thrust my hand away and stared at me. And the doubt did not fade.

I gave her glance for glance.

"Well, Arles?" I said.

Her lips quivered.

"It can't be. I know, but Lorryn is right. You know that; we can take no risks. To have the devil Ganelon back, after all that's happened, would be disastrous."

Devil, I thought. The devil Ganelon. Ganelon had hated the woodsfolk, yes. But now he had another, greater hatred. In his hour of weakness, the Coven had betrayed him. The woodsfolk could wait. Vengeance could not. It would be the devil Ganelon who would bring Caer Sécaire and the Castle crashing down about the ears of the Coven!

Which would mean playing a careful game!

"Yes, Lorryn is right," I said. "You've no way of knowing I'm not Ganelon. Perhaps you know it, Arles—" I smiled at her "—but there must be no chances taken. Let Lorryn test me."

"Well?" Lorryn said, looking at Arles.

Doubtfully she glanced from me to the bearded man.

"I—very well, I suppose."

Lorryn barked laughter.

"My tests might fail. But there is one who can see the truth. Freydis."

"Let Freydis test me," I said quickly, and was rewarded by seeing Lorryn hesitate.

"Very well," he said at last. "If I'm wrong, I'll apologize now. But if I'm right, I'll kill you, or try to. There's only one other life I'd enjoy taking the more, and the shape-changer isn't in my reach—yet."

Again Lorryn touched his scarred cheek. At the thought of Lord Matholch, warmth came into his gray eyes; a distant ember burned for an instant there. I had seen hatred before. But not often had I seen such hatred as Lorryn held for—the wolfling?

Well, let him kill Matholch, if he could! There was another, softer throat in which I wanted to sink my fingers. Nor could all her magic protect the red witch when Ganelon came back to Caer Sécaire, and broke the Coven like rotten twigs in his hands!

Again the black rage thundered up like a deluging tide. That fury had wiped out Edward Bond—but it had not wiped out Ganelon's cunning.

"As you like, Lorryn," I said quietly. "Let's go to Freydis now."

He nodded shortly. Lorryn on one side of me, Arles, puzzled and troubled, on the other, we moved up the valley, surrounded by the woodsfolk. The dazed slaves surged ahead.

The canyon walls closed in. A cave-mouth showed in the granite ahead.

We drew up in a rough semi-circle facing that cavern. Silence fell, broken by the whispering of leaves in the wind. The red sun was rising over the mountain wall.

Out of the darkness came a voice, deep, resonant, powerful.

"I am awake," it said. "What is your need?"

"Mother Freydis, we have helots captured from the Coven," Arles said quickly. "The sleep is on them."

"Send them to me."

Lorryn gave Arles an angry look. He pushed forward.

"Mother Freydis!" he called.

"I hear."

"We need your sight. This man, Edward Bond—I think he is Ganelon, came back from the Earth-world where you sent him."

There was a long pause.

"Send him in to me," the deep voice finally said. "But first the helots."

At a signal from Lorryn the woodsfolk began herding the slaves toward the cave-mouth. They made no resistance. Empty-eyed, they trooped toward that cryptic darkness and, one by one, vanished.

Lorryn looked at me and jerked his head toward the cavern. I smiled.

"When I come out, we shall be friends again as before," I said.

His eyes did not soften.

"Freydis must decide that."

I turned to Arles.

"Freydis shall decide," I said. "But there is nothing to fear, Arles. Remember that. I am not Ganelon."

She watched me, afraid, unsure, as I stepped back a pace or two.

The silent throng of woodsfolk stared, waiting warily. They had their weapons ready.

I laughed softly and turned.

I walked toward the cave-mouth.

The blackness swallowed me.

Strange to relate, I felt sure of myself as I walked up the sloping ramp in the darkness. Ahead of me, around a bend, I could see the glimmer of firelight, and I smiled. It had been difficult to speak with these upstart woodrunners as if they were my equals, as if I were still Edward Bond. It would be difficult to talk to their witchwoman as if she had as much knowledge as a Lord of the Coven. Some she must have, or she could never have managed the transfer which had sent me into the Earth-world and brought out Edward Bond. But I thought I could deceive her or anyone these rebels had to offer me.

The small cave at the turn of the corridor was empty except for Freydis. Her back was to me. She crouched on her knees before a small fire that burned, apparently without fuel, in a dish of crystal. She wore a white robe, and her white hair lay in two heavy braids along her back. I stopped, trying to feel like Edward Bond again, to determine what he would have said in this moment. Then Freydis turned and rose.

She rose tremendously. Few in the Dark World can look me in the eye, but Freydis' clear blue gaze was level with my own. Her great shoulders and great, smooth arms were as powerful as a man's, and if age was upon her, it did not show in her easy motions or in the timeless face she turned to me. Only in the eyes was knowledge mirrored, and I knew as I met them that she was old indeed.

"Good morning, Ganelon," she said in her deep, serene voice.

I gaped. She knew me as surely as if she read my mind. Yet I was sure, or nearly sure, that no one in the Dark World could do that. For a moment I almost stammered. Then pride came to my rescue.

"Good day, old woman," I said. "I come to offer you a chance for your life, if you obey me. We have a score to settle, you and I."

She smiled.

"Sit down, Covenanter," she said. "The last time we matched strength, you traded worlds. Would you like to visit Earth again, Lord Ganelon?"

It was my turn to laugh.

"You could not. And if you could, you wouldn't, after you hear me."

Her blue eyes searched mine.

"You want something desperately," she said in a slow voice. "Your very presence here, offering me terms, proves that. I never thought to see the Lord Ganelon face to face unless he was in chains or in a berserker battle-mood. Your need of me, Lord Ganelon, serves as chains for you now. You are fettered by your need, and helpless."

She turned back to the fire and sat down with graceful smoothness, her huge body under perfect control. Across the flame in its crystal bowl she faced me.

"Sit down, Ganelon," she said again, "and we will bargain, you and I. One thing first—do not waste my time with lies. I shall know if you tell the truth, Covenanter. Remember it."

I shrugged.

"Why should I bother with lies for such as you?" I said. "I have nothing to hide from you. The more of truth you know, the stronger you'll see my case is. First, though—those slaves who came in before me?"

She nodded toward the back of the cave.

"I sent them into the inner mountain. They sleep. You know the heavy sleep that conies upon those loosed from the Spell, Lord Ganelon."

I sat down, shaking my head.

"No—no, that I can not quite remember. I—you asked for the truth, old woman. Listen to it, then. I am Ganelon, but the false memories of Edward Bond still blur my mind. As Edward Bond I came here—but Arles told me one thing that brought Ganelon back. She told me that the Coven, in my hour of weakness, had dressed me in the blue cloak of the sacrifice and I was riding for Caer Sécaire when the woodsmen attacked us. Must I tell you now what my first wish in life is, witch-woman?"

"Revenge on the Coven." She said it hollowly, her eyes burning into mine through the fire. "This is the truth you speak, Covenanter. You want my help in getting your vengeance. What can you offer the woodsfolk in return, save fire and sword? Why should we trust you, Ganelon?"

Her ageless eyes burned into mine.

"Because of what you want. My desire is vengeance. Yours is—what?"

"The end of Llyr—the ruin of the Coven!" Her voice was resonant and her whole ageless face lighted as she spoke.

"So. I too desire the ruin of the Coven and the end—the end of Llyr." My tongue stumbled a little when I said that. I was not sure why. True, I had been sealed to Llyr in a great and terrible ceremony once—I could not recall that much. But Llyr and I were not one. We might have been, had events run differently. I shuddered now at the thought of it.

Yes, it was Llyr's end I desired now—must desire, if I hoped to live.

Freydis looked at me keenly. She nodded.

"Yes—perhaps you do. Perhaps you do. What do you want of us then, Ganelon?"

I spoke hastily:

"I want you to swear to your people that I am Edward Bond. No—wait! I can do more for them now than Edward Bond could do. Give thanks that I am Ganelon again, old woman! For only he can help you. Listen to me. Your foresters could not kill me. I know that. Ganelon is deathless, except on Llyr's altar. But they could fetter me and keep me prisoner here until you could work your spells again and bring Edward Bond back. And that would be foolish for your sake and for mine.

"Edward Bond has done all he knows for you. Now it's Ganelon's turn. Who else could tell you how Llyr is vulnerable, or where Matholch keeps his secret weapons, or how one can vanquish Edeyrn? These things I know—or I once knew. You must help me win my memories back, Freydis. After that—" I grinned fiercely.

She nodded. Then she sat quiet for a while.

"What do you want me to do, then, Ganelon?" she asked, at last.

"Tell me first about the bridging of the worlds," I said eagerly. "How did you change Edward Bond and me?"

Freydis smiled grimly.

"Not so fast, Covenanter!" she answered. "I have my secrets too! I will answer only a part of that question. We wrought the change, as you must guess, simply to rid ourselves of you. You must remember how fiercely you were pressing us in your raids for slaves, in your hatred of our freedom. We are a proud people, Ganelon, and we would not be oppressed forever. But we knew there was no death for you except in a way we could not use.

"I knew of the twin world of Earth. I searched, and found Edward Bond. And after much striving, much effort, I wrought a certain transition that put you in the other world, with the memories of Edward Bond blotting out your own.

"We were rid of you. True, we had Edward Bond with us, and we did not trust him either. He was too like you. But him we could kill if we must. We did not. He is a strong man, Covenanter. We came to trust him and rely upon him. He brought us new ideas of warfare. He was a good leader. It was he who planned the attack upon the next Coven sacrifice—"

"An attack that failed," I said. "Or would have failed, had I not swung my weight into the balance. Edward Bond had Earth-knowledge, yes. But his weapons and defenses could only have breached the outer walls of the Coven. You know there are powers, seldom used, but powers that do not fail!"

"I know," she said. "Yes, I know, Ganelon. Yet we had to try, at least. And the Coven had been weakened by losing you. Without you, none of the others would have dared call on Llyr, except perhaps Ghast Rhymi," She stared deeply into the fire. "I know you Ganelon. I know the pride that burns in your soul. And I know, too, that vengeance, now, would be very dear to your heart. Yet you were sealed to Llyr, once, and you have been Covenanter since your birth. How do I know you can be trusted?"

I did not answer that. And, after a moment, Freydis turned toward the smoke-blackened wall. She twitched aside a curtain I had not seen. There, in an alcove, was a Symbol, a very ancient Sign, older than civilization, older than human speech.

Yes, Freydis would be one of the few who knew what that Symbol meant. As I knew.

"Now will you swear that you speak with a straight tongue?" she said.

I moved my hand in the ritual gesture that bound me irrevocably. This was an oath I could not break without being damned and doubly damned, in this world and the next. But I had no hesitation. I spoke truth!

"I will destroy the Coven!" I said.

"And Llyr?"

"I will bring an end to Llyr!"

But sweat stood out on my forehead as I said that. It was not easy.

Freydis twitched the curtain back into place. She seemed satisfied.

"I have less doubt now," she said. "Well, Ganelon, the Norns weave strange threads together to make warp and woof of destiny. Yet there is a pattern, though sometimes we cannot see it. I did not ask you to swear fealty to the forest-folk."

"I realize that."

"You would not have sworn it," she said. "Nor is it necessary. After the Coven is broken, after an end is made to Llyr, I can guard the people of the woods against even you, Ganelon. And we may meet in battle then. But until then we are allies. I will name you—Edward Bond."

"I'll need more than that," I told her. "If the masquerade is to pass unchallenged."

"No one will doubt my word," Freydis said. Firelight flickered on her great frame, her smooth, ageless face.

"I cannot fight the Coven till I get back my memories. The memories of Ganelon. *All* of them."

She shook her head.

"Well," she said slowly, "I cannot do much on that score. Something, yes. But writing on the mind is touchy work, and memories, once erased, are not easily brought back. You still have Edward Bond's memories?"

I nodded.

"But my own, no. They're fragmentary. I know, for example, that I was sealed to Llyr, but the details I don't remember."

"It would be as well, perhaps, to let that memory stay lost," Freydis said somberly. "But you are right. A dulled tool is no use. So listen."

Rock-still, boulder-huge, she stood across the fire from me. Her voice deepened.

"I sent you into the Earth-world. I brought your double, Edward Bond, here. He helped us, and—Arles loved him, after a while. Even Lorryn, who does not trust many, grew to trust Edward Bond."

"Who is Lorryn?"

"One of us now. Not always. Years ago he had his cottage in the forest; he hunted, and few were as cunning as Lorryn in the chase. His wife was very young. Well, she died. Lorryn came back to his cottage one night and found death there, and blood, and a wolf that snarled at him from a bloody muzzle. He fought the wolf; he did not kill it. You saw Lorryn's cheek. His whole body is like that, scarred and wealed from wolf-fangs."

"A wolf?" I said. "Not—"

"A wolfling," Freydis said. "Lycanthrope, shape-changer. Matholch. Some day Lorryn will kill Matholch. He lives only for that."

"Let him have the red dog," I said contemptuously. "If he likes, I'll give him Matholch flayed!"

"Arles and Lorryn and Edward Bond have planned their campaign," Freydis said. "They swore that the last Sabbat had been celebrated in the Dark World. Edward Bond showed them new weapons he remembered from Earth. Such weapons have been built and are in the arsenal, ready. No Sabbats have been held since Medea and her followers went searching to Earth; the woodsfolk held their hands. There was nothing to strike at except old Ghast Rhymi. Now Medea and the rest of the Coven are back, they're ready. If you lead against them Ganelon, the Coven can be smashed, I think."

"The Coven has its own weapons," I muttered. "My memory fails—but I think Edeyrn has a power that—that—" I shook my head. "No, it's gone."

"How can Llyr be destroyed?" Freydis asked.

"I—I may have known once. Not now."

"Look at me," she said. And leaned forward, so that it seemed as though her ageless face was bathed in the fires.

Through the flames her gaze caught mine. Some ancient power kindled her clear blue eyes. Like pools of cool water under a bright sky—pools deep and unstirring, where one could sink into an azure silence forever and ever . . ..

As I looked the blue waters clouded, grew dark. I saw a great black dome against a black sky. I saw the thing that dwells deepest and most strongly in the mind of Ganelon—Caer Llyr!

The dome swam closer. It loomed above me. Its walls parted like dark water, and I moved in memory down the great smooth, shining corridor that leads to Llyr Himself.

Onward I moved. Faces flickered before me—Matholch's fierce grin. Edeyrn's cowled head with its glance that chilled, Medea's savage beauty that no man could ever forget, even in his hatred. They looked at me, mistrustfully. Their lips moved in soundless question. Curiously, I knew these were real faces I saw.

In the magic of Freydis' spell I was drifting through some dimensionless place where only the mind ventures, and I was meeting here the thoughts of the questing Coven, meeting the eyes of their minds. They knew me. They asked me fiercely a question I could not hear.

Death was in the face Matholch's mind turned to mine. All his hatred of me boiled furiously in his yellow wolf-eyes. His lips moved—almost I could hear him. Medea's features swam up before me, blotting out the shape-changer. Her red mouth framed a question—over and over.

"Ganelon, where are you? Ganelon my lover, where are you? You must come back to us. Ganelon!"

Edeyrn's faceless head moved between Medea and me, and very distantly I heard her cool, small voice echoing the same thought,

"You must return to us, Ganelon. Return to us and die!"

Anger drew a red curtain between those faces and myself.

Traitors, betrayers, false to the Coven oath! How dared they threaten Ganelon, the strongest of them all? How dared they— and why?

Why?

My brain reeled with the query. And then I realized there was one face missing from the Coven. These three had been searching the thought-planes for me, but what of Ghast Rhymi?

Deliberately I groped for the contact of his mind.

I could not touch him. But I remembered. I remembered Ghast Rhymi, whose face Edward Bond had never seen. Old, old, old, beyond good and evil, beyond fear and hatred, this was Ghast Rhymi, the wisest of the Coven. If he willed, he would answer my groping thought. If he willed not, nothing could force him. Nothing could harm the Eldest, for he lived only by force of his own will.

He could end himself instantly, by the power of a thought. And he is like a candle flame, flickering away as one grasps at him. life holds nothing more for him. He does not cling to it. If I had tried to seize him he could slip like fire or water from my grasp. He would as soon be dead as alive. But unless he must, he would not break his deep calm to think the thought that would change him into clay.

His mind and the image of his face remained hidden from my quest. He would not answer. The rest of the Coven still kept calling to me with a strange desperation in their minds—return and die, Lord Ganelon! But Ghast Rhymi did not care.

So I knew that it was at his command the death-sentence had been passed. And I knew I must seek him out and somehow force an answer from him—from Ghast Rhymi, upon whom all force was strengthless. Yet force him I must!

All this while my mind had been drifting effortlessly down the great hallway of Caer Llyr, borne upon that tide that flows deepest in the mind of Ganelon, the Chosen of Llyr—Ganelon, who must one day return to Him Who Waits. . . . As I was returning now.

A golden window glowed before me. I knew it for the window through which great Llyr looks out upon his world, the window through which he reaches for his sacrifices. And Llyr was hungry. I felt his hunger. Llyr was roaming the thought-planes too, and in the moment that I realized again where my mind was drifting, I felt suddenly the stir of a great reaching, a tentacular groping through the golden window.

Llyr had sensed my presence in the planes of his mind. He knew his Chosen. He stretched out his godlike grasp to fold me into that embrace from which there is no returning.

I heard the soundless cry of Medea, vanishing like a puff of smoke out of the thought-plane as she blanked her mind defensively from the terror. I heard Matholch's voiceless howl of pure fear as he closed his own mind. There was no sound from Edeyrn, but she was gone as utterly as if she had never thought a thought. I knew the three of them sat somewhere in their castle, eyes and minds closed tightly, willing themselves to blankness as Llyr roamed the thought-lanes seeking the food he had been denied so long.

A part of me shared the terror of the Coven. But a part of me re-membered Llyr. For an instant, almost I recaptured the dark ecstasy of that moment when Llyr and I were one, and the memory of horror and of dreadful joy came back, the memory of a power transcending all earthly things.

This was mine for the taking, if I opened my mind to Llyr. Only one man in a generation is sealed to Llyr, sharing in his godhead, exulting with him in the ecstasy of human sacrifice—and I was that one man if I chose to complete the ceremony that would make me Llyr's. If I chose, if I dared—ah!

The memory of anger came back. I must not release myself into that promised joy. I had sworn to put an end to Llyr. I had sworn by the Sign to finish the Coven and Llyr. Slowly, reluctantly, my mind pulled itself back from the fringing contact of those tentacles.

The moment that tentative contact was broken, a full tide of horror washed over me. Almost I had touched—*him*. Almost I had let myself be defiled beyond all human understanding by the terrible touch of—of—There is no word in any language for the thing that was Llyr. But I understood what had been in my mind as Edward Bond when I realized that to dwell on the same soil as Llyr, share the same life, was a defilement that made earth and life too terrible to endure—if one knew Llyr.

I must put an end to *him*. In that moment, I knew I must stand up and face the being we knew as Llyr and fight him to his end. No human creature had ever fully faced him—not even his sacrifices, not even his Chosen. But his slayer would have to face him, and I had sworn to be his slayer.

Shuddering, I drew back from the black depths of Caer Llyr, struggled to the surface of that still blue pool of thought which had been Freydis' eyes. The darkness ebbed around me and by degrees the walls of the cave came back, the fuelless flame, the great smooth-limbed sorceress who held my mind in the motionless deeps of her spell.

As I returned to awareness, slowly, slowly, knowledge darted through my mind in lightning-flashes, too swiftly to shape into words.

I knew, I remembered.

Ganelon's life came back in pictures that went vividly by and were printed forever on my brain. I knew his powers; I knew his secret strengths, his hidden weaknesses. I knew his sins. I exulted in his power and pride. I returned to my own identity and was fully Ganelon again. Or almost fully.

But there were still hidden things. Too much had been erased from my memory to come back in one full tide. There were gaps, and important gaps, in what I could recall.

The blue darkness cleared. I looked into Freydis' clear gaze across the fire. I smiled, feeling a cold and arrogant confidence welling up in me.

"You have done well, witch-woman," I told her.

"You remember?"

"Enough. Yes, enough." I laughed. "There are two trials before me, and the first is the easier of the two, and it is impossible. But I shall accomplish it."

"Ghast Rhymi?" she asked in a quiet voice.

"How do you know that?"

"I know the Coven. And I think, but I am not sure, that in Ghast Rhymi's hands lie the secrets of the Coven and of Llyr. But no man can force Ghast Rhymi to do his bidding."

"I'll find the way. Yes, I will even tell you what my next task is. You shall have the truth as I just learned it, witch. Do you know of the Mask and the Wand?"

Her eyes on mine, she shook her head. "Tell me. Perhaps I can help."

I laughed again. It was so fantastically implausible that she and I should stand here, sworn enemies of enemy clans, planning a single purpose together! Yet there was only a little I hid from her that day, and I think not very much that Freydis hid from me.

"In the palace of Medea, is a crystal mask and the silver Wand of Power," I told her. "What the Wand is I do not quite remember—yet. But when I find it, my hands will know. And with it I can overcome Medea and Matholch and all their powers. As for Edeyrn—well, this much I know. The Mask will save me from her."

I hesitated.

Medea I knew now. I knew the strange hungers and the strange thirsts that drove the beautiful red and white witch to her tryst-ings. I knew now, and shuddered a little to think of it, why she took her captives with those arrows of fire that did not kill at all, but only stunned them.

In the Dark World, my world, mutation has played strange changes upon flesh that began as human. Medea was one of the strangest of all. There is no word in Earth-tongues for it, because no creature such as Medea ever walked Earth. But there is an approximation. In reality perhaps, and certainly in legend, beings a little like her have been known on Earth. The name they give them is Vampire.

But Edeyrn, no. I could not remember. It may be that not even Ganelon had ever known. I only knew that in time of need, Edeyrn would uncover her face.

"Freydis," I said, and hesitated again. "What is Edeyrn?"

She shook her massive head, the white braids stirring on her shoulders.

"I have never known. I have only probed at her mind now and then, when we met as you met her today, on the thought-lanes. I have much power, Ganelon, but I have always drawn back from the chill I sensed beneath Edeyrn's hood. No, I cannot tell you what she is."

I laughed again. Recklessness was upon me now.

"Forget Edeyrn," I said. "When I have forced Ghast Rhymi to my bidding, and faced Llyr with the weapon that will end him, what shall I fear of Edeyrn? The Crystal Mask is the talisman against her. That much I know. Let her be whatever monstrous thing she wills—Ganelon has no fear of her."

"There is a weapon, then, against Llyr too?"

"There is a sword," I said. "A sword that is—is not quite a sword as we think of weapons. My mind is cloudy there still. But I know that Ghast Rhymi can tell me where it is. A weapon, yet not a weapon. The Sword Called Llyr."

For an instant, as I spoke that name, it seemed to me that the fire between us flickered as if a shadow had passed across its brightness. I should not have called the name aloud. An echo of it had gone ringing across the realms of thought, and in Caer Llyr perhaps Llyr Himself had stirred behind the golden window— stirred, and looked out.

Even here, I felt a faint flicker of hunger from that far-away domed place. And suddenly, I knew what I had done. *Llyr was awake!*

I stared at Freydis with widened eyes, meeting her blue gaze that was widening too. She must have felt the stir as It ran form-lessly all through the Dark World. In the Castle of the Coven I knew they had felt it too, perhaps that they looked at one another with the same instant dread which flashed between Freydis and me here.

Llyr was awake!

And I had wakened him. I had gone drifting in thought down that shining corridor and stood in thought before the very window itself, Llyr's Chosen, facing Llyr's living window. No wonder he had stirred at last to full awakening.

Exultation bubbled up in my mind.

"Now they must move!" I told Freydis joyfully. "You wrought better than you knew when you set my mind free to rove its old track. Llyr wakens and is hungrier than the Coven ever dared let him grow before. For overlong there has been no Sabbat, and Llyr ravens for his sacrifice. Have you spies watching the Castle now, witch-woman?"

She nodded.

"Good. Then we will know when the slaves are gathered again for a Sabbat meeting. It will be soon. It must be soon! And Edward Bond will lead an assault upon the Castle while the Coven are at Sabbat in Caer Sécaire. There will be the Mask and the Wand, old woman!" My voice deepened to a chant of triumph. "The Mask and the Wand for Ganelon, and Ghast Rhymi alone in the Castle to answer me if he can! The Norns fight on our side, Freydis!"

She looked at me long and without speaking.

Then a grim smile broke across her face and stooping, she spread her bare hand, palm down, upon the fuelless flame. I saw the fire lick up around her fingers. Deliberately she crushed it out beneath her hand, not flinching at all.

The fire flared and died away. The crystal dish stood empty upon its pedestal, and dimness closed around us. In that twilight the woman was a great figure of marble, towering beside me.

I heard her deep voice.

"The Norns are with us, Ganelon," she echoed. "See that you fight upon our side too, as far as your oath will take you. Or you must answer to the gods and to me. And by the gods—" she laughed harshly "—by the gods, if you betray me, I swear I'll smash you with no other power than this!"

In the dimness I saw her lift her great arms. We looked one another in the eye, this mighty sorceress and I, and I was not sure but that she could overcome me single combat if the need arose. By magic and by sheer muscle, I recognized an equal. I bent my head.

"So be it, Sorceress," I said, and we clasped hands there in the darkness. And almost I hoped I need not have to betray her.

Side by side, we went down the corridor to the cave mouth.

The half-circle of foresters still awaited us. Arles and the scarred Lorryn stood a little forward, lifting their heads eagerly as we emerged. I paused, catching the quiver of motion as calloused hands slipped stealthily toward hilt and bowstring. Panic, subdued and breathless, swept around the arc of woodsfolk.

I stood there savoring the moment of terror among them, knowing myself Ganelon and the nemesis that would bring harsh justice upon them all, in my own time. In my own good time.

But first I needed their help.

At my shoulder the deep voice of Freydis boomed through the glade.

"I have looked upon this man," she said. "I name him—Edward Bond."

Distrust of me fell away from them; Freydis' words reassured them.

Now the sap that runs through Ygdrasil-root stirred from its wintry sluggishness, and the inhuman guardians of the fate-tree roused to serve me. The three Norns—the Destiny-weavers—I prayed to them!

Urdur who rules the past!

She whispered of the Covenanters, and their powers and their weaknesses; of Matholch, the wolfling, whose berserk rages were his great flaw, the gap in his armor through which I could strike, when fury had drowned his wary cunning; of the red witch and of Edeyrn—and of old Ghast Rhymi. My enemies. Enemies whom I could destroy, with the aid of certain talismans that I had remembered now. Whom I would destroy!

Verdandi who rules the present!

Edward Bond had done his best. In the caves the rebels had showed me were weapons, crude rifles and grenades, gas-bombs and even a few makeshift flame-throwers. They would be useful against the Coven's slaves. How useless they would be against the Covenanters I alone knew. Though Freydis may have known too.

Yet Arles and Lorryn and their reckless followers were ready to use those Earth-weapons, very strange to them, in a desperate attack on the Castle. And I would give them that chance, as soon as our spies brought word of Sabbat-preparations. It would be soon. It would have to be soon. For Llyr was awake now—hungry, thirsting—beyond the Golden Window that is his door into the worlds of mankind.

Skuld who rules the future!

To Skuld I prayed most of all. I thought that the Coven would ride again to Caer Sécaire before another dawn came. By then I wanted the rebels ready.

Edward Bond had trained them well. There was military discipline, after a fashion. Each man knew his equipment thoroughly, and all were expert woodsmen. We laid our plans, Arles and Lorryn and I—though I did not tell them everything I intended— and group by group, the rebels slipped away into the forest, bound for the Castle.

They would not attack. They would not reveal themselves until the signal was given. Meantime, they would wait, concealed in the gulleys and scrub-woods around the Castle. But they would be ready. When the time came, they would ride down to the great gates. Their grenades would be helpful there.

Nor did it seem fantastic that we should battle magic with grenades and rifle. For I was beginning to realize more and more, as my memory slowly returned, that the Dark World was not ruled by laws of pure sorcery. To an Earth-mind such creatures as Matholch and Medea would have seemed supernatural, but I had a double mind, for as Ganelon I could use the memories of Edward Bond as a workman uses tools.

I had forgotten nothing I had ever known about Earth. And by applying logic to the Dark World, I understood things I had always before taken for granted.

The mutations gave the key. There are depths in the human mind forever unplumbed, potentialities for power as there are lost, atrophied senses—the ancient third eye that is the pineal gland. And the human organism is the most specialized thing of flesh that exists.

Any beast of prey is better armed with fang and claw. Man has only his brain. But as carnivores grew longer, more deadly talons, so man's mind developed correspondingly. Even in Earth-world there are mediums, mind-readers, psychomantic experts, ESP specialists. In the Dark World the mutations had run wild, producing cosmic abortions for which there might be no real need for another million years.

And such minds, with their new powers, would develop tools for those powers. The wands. Though no technician, I could understand their principle. Science tends toward simpler mechanisms; the klystron and the magnetron are little more than metal bars. Yet, under the right conditions, given energy and direction, they are powerful machines.

Well, the wands tapped the tremendous electromagnetic energy of the planet, which is, after all, simply a gargantuan magnet. As for the directive impulse, trained minds could easily supply that.

Whether or not Matholch actually changed to wolf-form, I did not know, though I did not think he did. Hypnosis was part of the answer. An angry cat will fluff out its fur and seem double its size. A cobra will, in effect, hypnotize its prey. Why? In order to break down the enemy's defenses, to disarm him, to weaken the single-purposiveness that is so vital in combat. No, perhaps Matholch did not turn into a wolf, but those under the spell of his hypnosis thought he did, which came to the same thing in the end.

Medea? There was a parallel. There are diseases in which blood transfusions are periodically necessary. Not that Medea drank blood; she had other thirsts. But vital nervous energy is as real a thing as a leucocyte, and, witch through she was, she did not need magic to serve her needs.

Of Edeyrn I was not so sure. Some stray remembrances hung like mists in my mind. Once I had known what she was, what chilling power lay hidden in the darkness of her cowl. And that was not magic either. The Crystal Mask would protect me against Edeyrn, but I knew no more than that.

Even Llyr—*even Llyr!* He was no god. That I knew well. Yet what he might be was something I could not even guess at as yet. Eventually I meant to find out, and the Sword Called Llyr, which was not a true sword, would aid me then.

Meanwhile, I had my part to play. Even with Freydis as my sponsor, I could not afford to rouse suspicion among the rebels. I had explained that Medea's drug had left me weak and shaken. That helped to explain any minor lapses I might make. Curiously, Lorryn seemed to have accepted me fully at Freydis' word, while in Arles' behavior I detected a faint, almost imperceptible reserve. I do not think that she suspected the truth. Or, if she did she was trying not to admit it, even in her own mind.

And I could not afford to let that suspicion grow.

The valley was very active now.

Much had happened since I came there in the dawn. I had been through enough exertion both physical and emotional to last an ordinary man for a week, but Ganelon had only begun his battle. It was thanks to Edward Bond that our plans for attack would be formulated so readily, and in a way I was glad I had been too busy for anything but the most impersonal planning with Arles and Lorryn.

It helped to cover the great gaps of my ignorance about things Edward Bond should know. Many times I angled craftily for information, many times I had to call upon the excuse of the mythical drug and upon the exhaustion of my ordeal at the Castle. But by the time our plans were laid, it seemed to me that even Arles' suspicions were partly lulled.

I knew I must lull them utterly.

We rose from the great map-table in the council-cavern. All of us were tired. I met Lorryn's scar-twisted grin, warmth in it now as he smiled at the man he thought his sworn friend, and I made Edward Bond's face smile back at him.

"We'll do it this time," I told him confidently. "This time we'll win!"

His smile twisted suddenly into a grimace, and the light like embers glowed in his deep eyes.

"Remember," he growled. "Matholch—for me!"

I looked down at the relief-map of the table, very skillfully made under Edward Bond's directions.

The dark green hills rolling with their strange forests of semi-animate trees, every brook traced in white plaster, every roadway marked. I laid my hand on the little mound of towers that was a miniature Castle of the coven. From it stretched the highway I had ridden last night, beside Medea, in my blue sacrificial robe. There was the valley and the windowless tower of Caer Sécaire which had been our destination.

For a moment I rode that highway again, in the darkness and the starshine, seeing Medea beside me in her scarlet cloak, her face a pale oval in the dusk, her mouth black-red, her eyes shining at me. I remembered the feel of that fiercely yielding body in my arms as I had held her last night, as I had held her so many times before. In my mind whirled a question.

Medea, Medea, red witch of Colchis, why did you betray me?

I ground my palm down on the tiny plaster towers of the Castle, feeling them powder away beneath my hand. I grinned fiercely at the ruin I had made of Edward Bond's model.

"We'll have no need for *this* again!" I said through my teeth.

Lorryn laughed.

"No need to repair it. Tomorrow the Coven Castle will be wreckage too."

I dusted the powdered plaster from my hand and looked across the table at the silent Arles. She looked at me gravely, waiting. I smiled.

"We haven't had a moment alone together," I said, making my voice tender. "I'll need sleep before I leave tonight, but there's time for a walk, if you'll come with me."

The grave green gaze dwelt upon mine. Then she nodded, without smiling, and came around the table, stretching out her hand to me. I took it and we went down the steps to the cave-mouth and out into the glen, neither of us speaking. I let her lead the way, and we walked in silence toward the upper end of the valley, the little stream tinkling away beside us.

Arles walked very lightly, her gossamer hair floating behind her in a pale misty veil. I wondered if it was by intent that she kept her free hand resting upon the holstered weapon at her side.

It was hard for me to keep my mind upon her, or to care whether or not she knew me for myself. Medea's face in all its beauty and its evil floated before me up the glen, a face no man who looked upon it could ever forget. For a moment I was angry at the recollection that Edward Bond, in my flesh, had taken last night the kisses she meant for Ganelon.

Well, I would see her again tonight, before she died by my hand!

In my mind I saw the tiny roadway of the map-table, winding down from Coven Castle to the sacrificial temple. Along the real road, sometime in the night to come, I knew the cavalcade would ride again as it had ridden with me last night. And again there would be forest men hiding along the road, and again I would lead them against the Coven. But this time the outcome would be very different from anything either the rebels or the Coven could expect.

What a strange web the Norns had woven! Last night as Edward Bond, tonight as Ganelon, I would lead the same men in the same combat against the same foe, but with a purpose as different as night from day.

The two of us, deadly enemies though we shared the same body in a strange, inverted way—enemies though we had never met and never could meet, for all our common flesh. It was an enigma too curious to unravel.

"Edward," a voice said at my shoulder. I looked down. Arles was facing me with the same enigmatic gaze I had met so often today. "Edward, is she very beautiful?"

I stared at her.

"Who?"

"The witch. The Coven witch. Medea."

I almost laughed aloud. Was this the answer to all her aloofness of the day? Did she think my own withdrawal, all the changes she sensed in me, were due to the charms of a rival beauty? Well, I must set her mind at rest about that, at any rate. I called upon Llyr to forgive me the lie, and I took her shoulders in my hands and said:

"There is no woman on this world or on Earth half so beautiful as you, my darling."

Still she looked up at me gravely.

"When you mean that, Edward, I'll be glad," she said. "You don't mean it now. I can tell. No." She put her fingers across my mouth as I began to protest. "Let's not talk about her now. She's a sorceress. She has powers neither of us can fight. It isn't your fault or mine that she's too beautiful to forget all in a moment. Never mind now. Look! Do you remember this place?"

She twisted deftly from my grasp and swept out a hand toward the panorama spread below us. We stood in a grove of tall, quivering trees high on the crest of the low mountain. The leaves and branches made a bower around us with their showers of shaking tendrils, but through an opening here and there we could see the rolling country far below us, glowing in the light of the red westering sun.

"This will be ours some day," said Arles softly. "After the Coven is gone, after Llyr has vanished. We'll be free to live above ground, clear the forests, build our cities—live like men again. Think of it, Edward! A whole world freed from savagery. And all because there were a few of us at the start who did not fear the Coven, and who found you. If we win the fight, Edward, it will be because of you and Freydis. We would have all been lost without you."

She turned suddenly, her pale gold hair flying out around her face like a halo of floating gauze, and she smiled at me with a sudden, bewitching charm I had never seen upon her face before.

Until now she had always turned a grave reserve to my advances. Now suddenly I saw her as Edward Bond had, and it came to me in a flash of surprise that Bond was a very fortunate man, after all. Medea's sultry scarlet beauty would never wholly vanish from my mind, I knew, but this Arles had her own delicate and delightful charm.

She was very near me, her lips parted as she smiled up into my face. For an instant I envied Edward Bond. Then I remembered. I *was* Edward Bond! But it was Ganelon who stooped suddenly and seized the forest girl in a fiercely ardent embrace that amazed her, for I felt her gasp of surprise against my breast and her stir of protest in the moment before my lips touched hers.

Then she protested no longer.

She was a strange, wild, shy little creature, very pleasant in my arms, very sweet to kiss. I knew by the way she responded to me that Edward Bond had never held her like this. But then Edward Bond was a weakling and a fool. And before the kiss had ended I knew where I would turn first for solace when Medea had paid for her treachery with her life. I would not forget Medea, but I would not soon forget this kiss of Aries', either.

She clung to me in silence for a moment, her gossamer hair floating like thistledown about us both, and above her head I looked out over the valley which she had seen in her mind's eyes peopled with free forest folk, dotted with their cities. I knew that dream would never come true.

But I had a dream of my own!

I saw the forest people toiling to raise my mighty castle here perhaps on this very mountaintop, a castle to dominate the whole countryside and the lands beyond it. I saw them laboring under my overseers to conquer still further lands. I saw my armies marching, my slaves in my fields and mines, my navies on the dark oceans of a world that might well be mine.

Arles should share it with me—for a while. For a little while.

"I will always love you!" I said at her ear in the voice of Edward Bond. But it was Ganelon's lips that found her lips in the one last ardent kiss I had time for then.

Curiously, it seemed to me, that it took Ganelon's kisses at last to convince her I was Edward Bond . . ..

After that, for a few hours I slept, snug in Edward Bond's cavern rooms, in his comfortable bed, his guards watching beside the door. I slept with the memory of his sweet forest girl in my arms, and the prospect of his kingdom and his bride before me when I woke. I think in the Earth-world, Edward Bond must have dreamed jealous dreams.

But my own dreams were bad. Llyr in his castle was awake and hungry, and the great, cold, writhing tendrils of his hunger coiled lazily through my mind as I slept. I knew they stirred through every mind in the Dark World that had senses to perceive them. I knew I must wake soon, or never. But first I must sleep and grow strong for the night's ordeal. Resolutely I shut Llyr from my thoughts, resolutely I shut away Arles.

It was Medea's red smile and sidelong sultry glance that went down with me into the caverns of slumber.

Quietly Lorryn and I crouched among the trees and looked out at the Castle of the Coven, aglitter with lights against the starry sky. This was the night! We both knew it, and we were both tense and sweating with a nervous exultation that made this waiting hard indeed.

All around us in the woods, unseen, we heard the tiny sounds that meant an army of forest people waited our signal. And this time they were here in force. I caught a glint of starlight now and then on rifle-barrels, and I knew that the rebels were armed to put up a good fight against the soldiers of the Coven.

Not, perhaps, too good a fight.

I did not care. They thought they were going to storm the Castle and the Coven by sheer force of arms. I knew their only purpose was to divert attention while I made my way into the Castle and found the secret weapons that would give me power over the Covenanters. While they were striking, I would make my way to Ghast Rhymi and learn what was essential for me to learn.

After that, I did not care. Many foresters would die. Let them. There would still be slaves aplenty for me when my hour came. And nothing could stop me now. The Norns fought with me; I could not fail . . ..

There was much activity within the Castle. Voices floated out to us in the still night air. Figures moved to and fro against the lights. Then great gates were flung open upon a burst of golden radiance and the outlines of many riders crowded against it. A procession was coming out.

I heard chains clash musically, and I understood. This time the sacrifices rode chained to their mounts, so that no siren voices from the wood could lure them away. I shrugged. Let them go to their death, then. Llyr must be fed while he lasted. Better these than Ganelon, offered at the Golden Window. We saw them go off down the dark road, their chains ringing.

That was Matholch—there on the tall horse. I knew his vulpine outlines, the lift of the cloak upon his shoulders. And I would have known him too because of the great start, quickly checked, that Lorryn made beside me.

I heard the breath whistle through his nostrils, and his voice grated in my ear.

"Remember! That is mine!"

Edeyrn went by, tiny on her small mount, and a breath of chill seemed to me to sweep the darkness as she passed.

Medea came!

When I could no longer make out her outlines in the distance, when her white robe was no more than a shimmer and her scarlet cloak had melted into the dark, I turned to Lorryn, my mind spinning, my plans already chaotic with change. For a new compulsion had come upon me, and I was not even trying to resist it.

I had not seen a sacrifice in Caer Sécaire. This was one of the blank places in my memory, and a dangerous blank. Until Ganelon remembered the Sabbat, until he watched Llyr accept the offerings through the Golden Window, he could not wholly trust himself to fight the Coven and Llyr. This was a gap that must be filled. And curiosity was suddenly very strong upon me. Curiosity—and could it be—the pull of Llyr?

"Lorryn, wait for me here," I whispered in the darkness. "We've got to make sure they enter Caer Sécaire, start the Sabbat. I don't want to attack until I'm sure. Wait for me."

He stirred protestingly, but I was away before he could speak. I was out upon the road and running softly and silently after that processional winding toward the valley and the Mass of St. Sécaire, which is the Black Mass. It seemed to me as I ran that the fragrance of Medea's perfume hung upon the air I breathed, and my throat choked with the passion of my hatred for her, and of my love.

"She shall be the first to die," I promised myself in the dark. ... .

I watched the great iron doors of Caer Sécaire swing shut upon the last of the procession. The Caer was dark inside. They went quietly in, one by one, and vanished into the deeper night within. The doors clanged resonantly after them.

Some memory of Ganelon's, buried beneath the surface of conscious thought, urged me to the left, around the curve of the great wall. I followed the impulse obediently, moving almost like a sleep-walker toward a goal I did not know. Memory took me close under the looming rampart, made me lay my hands on its surface. There were heavy scrollings of pattern there, writhing like tendrils over the dark walls. My remembering fingers traced the curves, though my mind still wondered.

Then the wall moved beneath my hands. The scroll-work had been a key of sorts, and a door sank open in the blackness before me. I went confidently forward, out of black night, through a black door into deeper blackness within. But my feet knew the way.

A stairway rose beneath me in the dark. My feet had expected it and I did not stumble. It was very curious to move so blindly through this strange and dangerous place, not knowing where or why I moved, yet trusting my body to find the way. The stairs wound up and up.

Llyr was here. I could feel his hungry presence like a pressure on the mind, but many times intensified because of the narrow spaces within these walls, as if he were a sound of thunder reverberating again and again from the enclosed spaces of the Caer. Something within me reverberated soundlessly in answer, a roar of exultation that I suppressed in quick revolt.

Llyr and I were no longer linked by that ceremony of long ago. I repudiated it. I was not Llyr's Chosen now. But within me a sense I could not control quivered with ecstasy at the thought of those sacrifices who had fled blindly through the great doors of Caer Sécaire. And I wondered if the Coven—if Medea—thought of me now, who had so nearly stood with the sacrifices last night.

My feet paused upon the stairs. I could see nothing, but I knew that before me was a wall carved with scroll-patterns. My hands found it, traced the raised designs. A section of darkness slid sidewise and I was leaning upon a wide ledge, looking down, very far down.

Caer Sécaire was like a mighty grove of columns whose capitals soared up and up into infinite darkness. Somewhere above, too high for me to see its source, a light was beginning to glow. My heart paused when I saw it, for I knew that light—that golden radiance from a Golden Window.

Memory came fitfully back to me. The Window of Llyr. The Window of the Sacrifice. I could not see it, but my mind's eye remembered its glow. In Caer Llyr that Window's substance shone eternally, and Llyr Himself lolled behind it—far behind it—forever. But in Caer Sécaire and in the other temples of sacrifice that had once dotted the Dark World, there were replicas of the Window which glowed only when Llyr came bodilessly through the dark to take his due.

Above us, hovering and hungry, Llyr was dawning now in that golden radiance, like a sun in the night time of the temple. Where the Window of Sécaire was located, how it was shaped, I still could not remember. But something in me knew that golden light and shivered in response as I watched its brilliance strengthen through the columns of the temple.

Far below me I saw the Coven standing, tiny figures foreshortened to wedges of colored cloak—green-robed Matholch, yellow-robed Edeyrn, red Medea. Behind them stood a circle of guardsmen. Before them, as I watched, the last of the chosen slaves moved blindly away among the columns. I could not see where they were going, but in essence I knew. The Window was yawning for its sacrifices and somehow they must make their way to it.

As the light broadened, I saw that before the Coven stood a great cup-shaped altar, black on a black dais. Above it a lipped spout hung. My eyes traced the course of the trough which ended in the spout, and I saw now that there was a winding, descending curve, dark against the growing light, which came down in a great sweep from the mysterious heights overhead, stretching from—the Window?—to the cupped altar. A stir deep within me told me what that trough was for. I leaned upon the sill, shaking with an anticipation that was half for myself and half for Him, who hovered above us in the sun-like dawning of golden light.

Thinly from below me rose a chant. I knew Medea's voice, clear and silver, a thread of sound in the dimness and the silence. It rose like incense, quivering among the mighty, topless columns of Sécaire.

A tenseness of waiting grew and grew in the dim air of the temple. The figures below me stood motionless, heads lifted, watching the dawning light. Medea's voice chanted on and on.

Time paused there in the columned grove of Sécaire, while Llyr hovered above us waiting for his prey.

Then a thin and terrible cry rang out from the heights overhead. One scream. The light shot out blindingly in a great burst of exultation, like a voiceless answering cry from Llyr Himself. Medea's chant rose to a piercing climax and paused.

There was a stir among the columns; something moved along that curve of trough. My eyes sought the altar and the lipped spout above it.

The Coven was rigid, a cluster of frozen figures, waiting.

Blood began to drip from the spout.

I do not know long I hung there on the ledge, my eyes riveted to the altar. I do not know how many times I heard a cry ring out from above, how many times Medea's chant rose to a hungry climax as the light burst forth in a glory overhead and blood gushed into the great cup of the altar. I was deaf and blind to everything but this. I was half with Llyr at his Golden Window, shaken with ecstasy as he took his sacrifices, and half with the Coven below, glorying in their share of the ceremony of the Sabbat.

But I know I waited too long.

What saved me I do not know now. Some voice of the ego crying unheard in my mind that this was time dangerously spent, that I must be elsewhere before the Sabbat ended, that Lorryn and his men waited endlessly while I hung here battening like a glutton upon Llyr's feast.

Reluctantly awareness returned to my mind. With an infinite effort I pulled myself back from the brink of that Golden Window and stood reeling in the darkness, but in my own body again, not hovering mindlessly with Llyr in the heights above. The Coven was still tense below me, gripped in the ecstasy of the sacrifice. But for how long I could not be sure. Perhaps for the rest of the night; perhaps for only an hour. I must hurry, if hurrying were not already futile. There was no way to know.

So I went back in the darkness, down the unseen stairs. And out of the dark, unseen door, and back along the road to Coven Castle, my mind still reeling with remembered ecstasy, the glow of the Window still before my dazzled eyes, and the scarlet runnel above the altar, and the thin, sweet chanting of Medea louder in my ears than the sound of my own feet upon the road . . ..

The red moon was far down the sky when I came back to Lorryn, still crouching beside the castle wall and half mad with impatience. There was an eager stir among the unseen soldiers as I came running down the road, a forward surge as if they had waited to the very limit of endurance and would attack now whether I gave the word or no.

I waved to Lorryn while I was still twenty feet away, I was careless now of the Castle guardsmen. Let them see me. Let them hear.

"Give the signal!" I shouted to Lorryn. "Attack!"

I saw him start up beside the road, and the moonlight glinted upon the silver horn he lifted to his lips. Its blare of signal notes ripped the night to tatters. It ripped away the last of my lethargy too.

I heard the long yell that swept the forest as the woodsmen surged forward to the attack, and my own voice roared unbidden in reply, an ecstasy of battle-hunger that matched the ecstasy I had just shared with Llyr.

The rattle of rifle-fire drowned out our voices. The first explosions of grenades shook the Castle, outlining the outer walls in livid detail. There were shouts from within, wild trumpeting of signal horns, the cries of confused guardsmen, leaderless and afraid. But I knew they would rally. They had been trained well enough by Matholch and by myself. And they had weapons that could give the woodsmen a stiff fight.

When they recovered from this panic there would be much blood spilled around the outer walls.

I did not wait to see it. The first explosions had breached the barriers close beside me, and I scrambled recklessly through the gap, careless of the rifle fire that spattered against the stones. The Norns were with me tonight. I bore a charmed life, and I knew I could not fail.

Somewhere above me in the besieged towers Ghast Rhymi sat wrapped in his chill indifference, aloof as a god above the struggle around Coven Castle. I had a rendezvous with Ghast Rhymi, though he did not know it yet.

I plunged into the gateway of the Castle, heedless of the milling guards. They did not know me in the darkness and the confusion, but they knew by my tunic I was not a forester, and they let me shoulder them aside.

Three steps at a time, I ran up the great stairway.

Castle of the Coven! How strange it looked to me as I went striding through its halls. Familiar, yet curiously unknown, as though I saw it through the veil of Edward Bond's transplanted memories.

So long as I went rapidly, I seemed to know the way. But if I hesitated, my conscious mind took over control, and that mind was still clouded with artificial memories, so that I became confused in the halls and corridors which were familiar to me when I did not think directly of them.

It was as if whatever I focused on sharply receded into unfamiliarity while everything else remained clear, until I thought of it.

I strode down hallways arched overhead and paved underfoot in bright, intricate mosaics that told legendary tales half-familiar to me. I walked upon centaurs and satyrs whose very faces were well known to the Ganelon half of my mind, while the Edward Bond half wondered in vain whether such people had really lived in this distorted world of mutations.

This double mind at times was a source of strength to me, and at others a source of devouring weakness. Just now I hoped fervently that I might meet no delays for once I lost this rushing thread of memory which was leading me toward Ghast Rhymi, I might never find it again. Any interruption might be fatal to my plans.

Ghast Rhymi, my memories told me, would be somewhere in the highest tower of the castle. There too would be the treasure-room where the Mask and the Wand lay hidden, and hidden deeper in the serene, untouchable thoughts of Ghast Rhymi, lay the secret of Llyr's vulnerability.

These three things I must have, and the getting would not be easy. For I knew—without clearly remembering how or by what— that the treasure-room was guarded by Ghast Rhymi. The Coven would not have left open to all comers that secret place where the things that could end them lay hidden.

Even I, even Ganelon, had a secret thing locked in that treasury. For no Covenanter, no warlock, no sorceress can deal in the dark powers without creating, himself, the one instrument that can destroy him. This is the Law.

There are secrets behind it which I may not speak of, but the common one is clear. All Earth's folklore is rife with the same legend. Powerful men and women must focus their power in an object detached from themselves.

The myth of the external soul is common on all Earth races, but the reason for it lies deep in the lore of the Dark World. This much I can say—that there must be a balance in all things. For every negative, a positive. We of the Coven could not build up our power without creating a corresponding weakness somewhere, somehow, and we must hide that weakness so cunningly that no enemy could find it.

Not even the Coven knew wherein my own secret lay. I knew Medea's, and I knew Edeyrn's only partially, and as for Matholch—well, against him I needed only my own Covenanter strength. Ghast Rhymi did not matter. He would not bother to fight.

But Llyr? Ah!

Somewhere the Sword lay hidden, and he who could find and use it in that unknown way for which it was fashioned, he held the existence of Llyr in his own hand. But there was danger. For as Llyr's power in the Dark World was beyond imagination, so too must be that balancing power hidden in the Sword. Even to go near it might be fatally dangerous. To hold it in the hand— well, hold it I must, and there was no profit in thinking about danger.

I went up and up, on and on.

I could not hear the sounds of battle. But I knew that at the gate the Coven guards and slaves were fighting and falling, as Lorryn's men, too, were falling. I had warned Lorryn that none must break through his lines to warn those at Caer Sécaire. I knew that he would follow that order, despite his anxiety to come to grips with Matholch. For the rest, there was one in the Castle who could, without stirring, send a message to Medea. One person!

He had not sent that message. I knew that as I thrust through the white curtain and came out into the tower room. The little chamber was semicircular, walls, floor and ceiling were ivory pale. The casement windows were shut, but Ghast Rhymi had never needed sight to send out his vision.

He sat there, an old, old man, relaxed amid the cushions of his seat, snowy hair and beard falling in curled ringlets that blended with his white, plain robe. His hands lay upon the chair-arms, pale as wax, so transparent that I could almost trace the course of the thinned blood that stirred so feebly in those old veins.

Wick and wax had burned down. The flame of life flickered softly, and a wind might send that flame into eternal darkness. So sat the Ancient of Days, his blind blue gaze not seeing me, but turned upon inward things.

Ganelon's memories flooded back. Ganelon had learned much from Ghast Rhymi. Even then, the Covenanter had been old. Now the tides of time had worn him, as the tides of the sea wear a stone till nothing is left but a thin shell, translucent as clouded glass.

Within Ghast Rhymi I could see the life-fires dwindling, sunk to embers, almost ash.

He did not see me. Not easily can Ghast Rhymi be drawn back from the deeps where his thoughts move.

I spoke to him, but he did not answer.

I went past him then, warily, toward the wall that divided the tower-top into two halves. There was no sign of a door, but I knew the combination. I moved my palms in an intricate pattern on the cool surface, and a gap widened before me.

I crossed the threshold.

Here were kept the holy things of the Coven.

I looked upon that treasure-vault with new eyes, clearer because of Edward Bond's memories. That lens, burning with dull amber lights there in its hollowed place in the wall—I had never wondered much about it before. It killed. But memories of Earth-science told me why. It was not magic, but an instantaneous drainage of the electrical energy of the brain. And that conical black device—that killed, too. It could shake a man to pieces, by shuttling his life-force back and forth so rapidly between artificial cathode and anode that living flesh could not stand the strain. Alternating current, with variations!

But these weapons did not interest me now. I sought other loot. There was no death-traps to beware of, for none but the Coven knew the way to enter this treasure-room, or its location, or even that it existed, save the legends. And no slave or guard would have dared to enter Ghast Rhymi's tower.

My gaze passed over a sword, but not the one I needed; a burnished shield; a harp, set with an intricate array of manual controls. I knew that harp. Earth has legends of it—the harp of Orpheus, that could bring back the dead from Hades. Human hands could not play it. But I was not quite ready for the harp, yet.

What I wanted lay on a shelf, sealed in its cylindrical case. I broke open the seals and took out the thin black rod with its hand-grip.

The Wand of Power. The Wand that could tap the electro-magnetic force of a planet. So could other wands of this type—but this was the only one without the safety-device that limited its power. It was dangerous to use.

In another case I found the Crystal Mask—a curved, transparent plate that shielded my eyes like a domino mask of glass. This mask would shield one from Edeyrn.

I searched further. But of the Sword of Llyr I could find no trace.

Time did not lag. I heard nothing of the noise of battle, but I knew that the battle went on, and I knew, too, that sooner or later the Coven would return to the Castle. Well, I could fight the Coven now, but I could not fight Llyr. I dared not risk the issue till I had made sure.

In the door of the vault I stood, staring at Ghast Rhymi's silvery head. Whatever guardian thought he kept here, knew I had a right to the treasure room. He made no motion. His thoughts moved far out in unimaginable abysses, nor could they be easily drawn back. And it was impossible to put pressure on Ghast Rhymi. He had the prefect answer. He could die.

Well, I too had an answer!

I went back to the vault and lifted the harp. I carried it out and set it down before the old man. No life showed in his blue stare.

I went to the windows and flung them open. Then I returned, dropping to the cushions beside the harp, and lightly touched its intricate controls.

That harp had been in the Earth-world, or others like it. Legends know its singing strings, as legends tell of mystic swords. There was the lyre of Orpheus, strong with power, that Jupiter placed amid the stars. There was the harp of Gwydion of Britain, that charmed the souls of men. And the harp of Alfred, that helped to crush Daneland. There was David's harp that he played before Saul.

Power rests in music. No man today can say what sound broke the walls of Jericho, but once men knew.

Here in the Dark World this harp had its legends among the common folk. Men said that a demon played it, that the airy fingers of elemental spirits plucked at its strings. Well, in a way they were right.

For an incredible perfection of science had created this harp. It was a machine. Sonic, sub-sonic, and pure vibration to match the thought-waves emitted by the brain blended into a whole that was party hypnosis and part electric magnetism. The brain is a colloid, a machine, and any machine can be controlled.

And the harp of power could find the key to a mind, and lay bonds upon that mind.

Through the open windows, faintly from below, I heard the clash of swords and the dim shouts of fighting men. But these sounds did not touch Ghast Rhymi. He was lost on the plane of pure abstraction, thinking his ancient, deep thoughts.

My fingers touched the controls of the harp, awkwardly at first, then with more ease as manual dexterity came back with memory.

The sigh of a plucked string whispered through the white room. The murmuring of minor notes, in a low, dreamily distant key. And as the machine found the patterns of Ghast Rhymi's mind, under my hands the harp quickened into breathing life.

The soul of Ghast Rhymi—translated into terms of pure music!

Shrill and ear-piercing a single note sang. Higher and higher it mounted, fading into inaudibility. Deep down a roaring, windy noise began, rising and swelling into the demon-haunted shout of a gale. Rivers of air poured their music into the threnody.

High—high—cold and pure and white as the snowy summit of a great mountain, that single thin note sang and sang again.

Louder grew the great winds. Rippling arpeggios raced through the rising torrent of the sorcerous music.

Thunder of riven rocks—shrill screaming of earthquake-shaken lands—yelling of a deluge that poured down upon tossing forests.

A heavy humming note, hollow and unearthy, and I saw the gulfs between the worlds where the empty night of space makes a trackless desert.

And suddenly, incongruously, a gay lilting tune, with an infectious rocking rhythm, that brought to my mind bright colors and sunlit streams and fields.

Ghast Rhymi stirred.

For an instant awareness came back into his blue eyes. He saw me.

And I saw the life-fires sink within that frail, ancient body.

I knew that he was dying—that I had troubled his long peace— that he had relinquished his casual hold upon life.

I drew the harp toward me. I touched the controls.

Ghast Rhymi sat before me, dead, the faintest possible spark fading within that old brain.

I sent the sorcerous spell of the harp blowing like a mighty wind upon the dying embers of Ghast Rhymi's life.

As Orpheus drew back the dead Eurydice from Pluto's realm, so I cast my net of music, snared the soul of Ghast Rhymi, drew him back from death!

He struggled at first, I felt his mind turn and writhe, trying to escape, but the harp had already found the key to his mind, and it would not let him go. Inexorably it drew him.

The ember flickered—faded—brightened again.

Louder sang the strings. Deeper roared the tumult of shaking waters.

Higher the white, shrill note, pure as a star's icy light, leaped and ever rose.

Roaring, racing, sweet with honey-musk, perfumed with flower-scent and ambergris, blazing with color, opal and blood-ruby and amethyst-blue, that mighty tapestry of color rippled and shook like a visible web of magic through the room.

The web reached out.

Swept around Ghast Rhymi like a fowler's snare!

Back in those faded blue eyes the light of awareness grew. He had stopped struggling. He had given up the fight. It was easier to come back to life—to let me question him—than to battle the singing strings that could cage a man's very soul.

Under the white beard the old man's lips moved.

"Ganelon," he said. "I knew—when the harp sang—who played it. Well, ask your questions. And then let me die. I would not live in the days that are coming now. But you will live, Ganelon—and yet you will die too. That much I have read in the future."

The hoary head bent slowly. For an instant Ghast Rhymi listened—and I listened too.

The last, achingly sweet notes of the harp died upon the trembling air.

Through the open windows came the muted clash of swords and the wordless shriek of a dying man.

Pity flooded me. The shadow of greatness that had cloaked Ghast Rhymi was gone. He sat there, a shrunken, fragile old man, and I felt a momentary unreasoning impulse to turn on my heel and leave him to drift back into his peaceful abyss of thought. Once, I remembered, Ghast Rhymi had seemed a tall, huge figure—though he had never been that in my lifetime. But in my childhood I had sat at the feet of this Covenanter and looked up with awe at the majestic, bearded face with reverence.

Perhaps there had been more life in that face then, more warmth and humanity. It was remote now. It was like the face of god, or of one who had looked upon too many gods.

My tongue stumbled.

"Master," I said. "I am sorry!"

No light came into the distant blue gaze, yet I sensed a stirring.

"You name me master?" he said. "You—Ganelon? It has been a long time since you humbled yourself to anyone."

The taste of my triumph was ashes. I bowed my head. Yes, I had conquered Ghast Rhymi, and I did not like the savor of that conquest.

"In the end the circle completes itself," the old man said quietly. "We are more kin than the others. Both you and I are human, Ganelon, not mutants. Because I am Leader of the Coven I let Medea and the others use my wisdom. But—but—" He hesitated.

"For two decades my mind has dwelt in shadow," he went on. "Beyond good and evil, beyond life and the figures that move like puppets on the stream of life. When I was wakened, I would give the answers I knew. It did not matter. I had thought that I had lost all touch with reality. And that if death swept over every man and woman in the Dark World, it would not matter."

I could not speak. I knew that I had done Ghast Rhymi a very great wrong in wakening him from his deep peace.

The blue stars dwelt on me.

"And I find that it does matter, after all. No blood of mine runs in your veins, Ganelon. Yet we are kin. I taught you, as I would have taught my own son. I trained you for your task—to rule the Coven in my place. And now, I think I regret many things. Most of all the answer I gave the Covenanters after Medea brought you back from Earth-world."

"You told them to kill me," I said.

He nodded.

"Matholch was afraid. Edeyrn sided with him. They made Medea agree. Matholch said, 'Ganelon is changed. There is danger. Let the old man read the future and see what it holds.' So they came to me, and I let my mind ride the winds of time and see what lay ahead."

"And that was—?"

"The end of the Coven," Ghast Rhymi said. "If you lived. I foresaw the arms of Llyr reaching into the Dark World, and Matholch lying dead in a shadowed place, and doom upon Edeyrn and Medea. For time is fluid, Ganelon. It changes as men change. The probabilities alter. When you went into Earth-world, you were Ganelon. But you came back with a double mind. You have the memories of Edward Bond, which you can use as tools. Medea should have left you in Earth-world. But she loved you."

"Yet she agreed to let them kill me," I said.

"Do you know what was in her thoughts?" Ghast Rhymi asked. "In Caer Sécaire, at the time of sacrifice, Llyr would come. And you have been sealed to Llyr. Did Medea think you could be killed, then?"

A doubt grew within me. But Medea had led me, like a sheep to slaughter, in the procession to the Caer. If she could justify herself, let her. I knew that Edeyrn and Matholch could not.

"I may let Medea live, then," I said. "But not the wolfling. I have already promised his life. And as for Edeyrn, she must perish."

I showed Ghast Rhymi the Crystal Mask. He nodded.

"But Llyr?"

"I was sealed to Him as Ganelon," I said. "Now you say I have two minds. Or, at least, an extra set of memories, even though they are artificial. I am not willing to be liege to Llyr! I learned many things in the Earth-world. *Llyr is no god!*"

The ancient head bent. A transparent hand rose and touched the ringlets of the beard. Then Ghast Rhymi looked at me, and he smiled.

"So you know that, do you?" he asked. "I will tell you something, Ganelon, that no one else has guessed. You are not the first to come from Earth-world to the Dark World. I was the first."

I stared at him with unconcealed amazement.

"And you were born in the Dark World; I was not," he said. "My flesh sprang from the dust of Earth. It has been very long since I crossed, and I can never return now, for my span is long outlived. Only here can I keep the life-spark burning within me, though I do not much care about that either. Yet I am Earth-born, and I knew Vortigern and the kings of Wales. I had my own holdings at Caer-Merdin, and a different sun from this red ember in the Dark World's sky shone upon Caer-Merdin! Blue sky, blue sea of Britain, the gray stones of the Druid altars under the oak forests. That is my home, Ganelon. *Was* my home. Until my science, that men in those days called magic, brought me here, with a woman's aid. A Dark-World woman named Viviane."

"You are Earth-born?" I said.

"Once—yes. As I grew older here, very, very old, I regretted my exile. I had acquired enough of wisdom. I would have changed it all for one breath of the cool, sweet air that blew in from the Irish Sea when I was a boy. But never could I return. My body would fall to dust in the Earth-world. So I lost myself in dreams—dreams of Earth, Ganelon."

His blue eyes brightened with memories.

His voice deepened.

"In my dreams I brought back the old days. I stood again on the crags of Wales, watching the salmon leaping in the waters of gray Usk. I saw Artorius again, and his father Uther, and I smelled the old smells of Britain in her youth. But they were dreams!

"And dreams are not enough. For the sake of the love I bore the dust from which I sprang, for the sake of a wind that blew from ancient Ireland, I will help you now, Ganelon. I had never thought that life would matter to me any more. But that these abominations should lead a man of Earth to slaughter—no! And man of Earth you are now, though born on this world of sorcery!"

He leaned forward, compelling me with his gaze.

"You are right. Llyr is no god. He is—a monster. No more then that. And he can be slain."

"With the Sword Called Llyr?"

"Listen. Put these legends out of your mind. That is Llyr's power, and the power of the Dark World. All is veiled in mystic symbols of terror. But behind the veil lies simple truth. Vampire, werewolf, upas-tree—they all are biological freaks, mutations run wild! And the first mutation was Llyr. His birth split the one time-world into two, each spinning along its line of probability. He was a key factor in the temporal pattern of entropy.

"Listen again. At birth, Llyr was human. But his mind was not as the minds of others. He had certain natural powers, latent powers, which ordinarily would not have developed in the race for a million years. Because they did develop in him too soon, they were warped and distorted, and put to evil ends. In the future world of logic and science, his mental powers would have fitted. In the dark times of superstition, they did not fit too well. So he developed, with the science at his command and the mental strength he had, into a monster.

"Human once. Less human as he grew older and wiser in his alien knowledge. In Caer Llyr are machines which sent out certain radiations necessary to the existence of Llyr. Those radiations permeate the Dark World. They have caused other mutations, such as Matholch and Edeyrn and Medea.

"Kill Llyr and his machines will stop. The curse of abnormal mutations will be lifted. The shadow over this planet will be gone."

"How may I kill Him?" I asked.

"With the Sword Called Llyr. His life is bound up with that Sword, as a machine is dependent on its parts. I am not certain of the reason for this, Ganelon, but Llyr is not human—now. He is part machine and part pure energy and part something unimaginable. But he was born of flesh, and he must maintain his contact with the Dark World, or die. The Sword is his contact."

"Where is the Sword?"

"At Caer Llyr," Ghast Rhymi said, "Go there. By the altar, there is a crystal pane. Don't you remember?"

"I remember."

"Break that pane. Then you will find the Sword Called Llyr."

He sank back. His eyes closed, then opened again.

I knelt before him and he made the Ancient Sign above me.

"Strange," he murmured, half to himself. "Strange that I should send a man to battle again, as I sent so many, long ago."

The white head bent forward. Snowy beard lay upon the snowy robe.

"For the sake of a wind that blew from Ireland," the old man whispered.

Through the open windows a breath of air drifted, gently ruffling the white ringlets of hair and beard . . ..

The winds of the Dark World stirred in the silent room, paused—and were gone!

Now, indeed, I stood alone . . ..

From Ghast Rhymi's chamber I went down the tower steps and into the courtyard.

The battle was nearly over. Scarcely a score of the Castle's defenders were still on their feet. Around them Lorryn's pack ravened and yelled. Back to back, grimly silent, the dead-eyed guardsmen wove their blades in a steel mesh that momentarily held at bay their attackers.

There was no time to be wasted here. I caught sight of Lorryn's scarred face and made for him. He showed me his teeth in a triumphant grin.

"We have them, Bond."

"It took you long enough," I said. "These dogs must be slain quickly!" I caught a sword from a nearby woodsman.

Power flowed up the blade and into the hilt—into me.

I plunged into the thick of the battle. The foresters made way for me. Beside me Lorryn laughed quietly.

Then I came face to face with a guardsman. His blade swung up in thrust and parry, and I twisted aside, so that his steel sang harmlessly through the air. My sword-point leaped like a striking snake for his throat. The shock of metal grating on bone jarred my wrist.

I tore the weapon free and glimpsed Lorryn, still grinning, engaging another of the guardsmen.

"Kill them!" I shouted. "Kill them!"

I did not wait for response. I went forward against the blind-eyed soldiers of Medea, slashing, striking, thrusting, as though these men were the Coven, my enemies! I hated each blankly staring face. Red tides of rage began to surge up, narrowing my vision and clouding my mind with hot mists.

For a few moments I was drunk with the lust for killing.

Lorryn's hands gripped my shoulders. His voice came. "Bond! *Bond!*"

The fogs were swept away. I stared around. Not one of the guardsmen was left alive. Bloody, hacked corpses lay sprawled on the gray flagstone of the courtyard. The woodsmen, panting hard, were wiping their blades clean.

"Did any escape to carry warning to Caer Sécaire?" I asked.

Despite his perpetual scarred grin, Lorryn looked troubled.

"I'm not sure. I don't think so, but the place is a rabbit-warren."

"The harm's done then," I said. "We hadn't enough men to throw a cordon around the Castle."

He grimaced. "Warned or not, what's the odds? We can slay the Covenanters as we killed their guards."

"We ride to Caer Llyr," I said, watching him.

I saw the shadow of fear in the cold gray eyes. Lorryn rubbed his grizzled beard and scowled.

"I don't understand. Why?"

"To kill Llyr."

Amazement battled with ancient superstitious terror in his face. His gaze searched mine and apparently read the answer he wanted.

"To kill—*that?*"

I nodded. "I've seen Ghast Rhymi. He told me the way."

The men around us were watching and listening. Lorryn hesitated.

"We didn't bargain for this," he said. "Yet by the gods! To kill *Llyr!*"

Suddenly he sprang into action, shouting orders. Swords were sheathed. Men ran to untether the mounts. Within minutes we were in our saddles, riding out from the courtyard, the shadow of the Castle falling heavily upon us till the moon lifted above the tallest tower.

I rose in my stirrups and looked back. Up there, dead, sat Ghast Rhymi, first of the Coven to die by my hand. I had killed him as surely as if I had plunged steel into his heart.

I dropped back into the saddle, pressing heels into my horse's flanks. He bolted forward. Lorryn urged his steed level with me. Behind us the woodsmen strung out in a long uneven line as we galloped across the low hills toward the distant mountains. It would be dawn before we could reach Caer Llyr. And there was no time to waste.

Medea and Edeyrn and Matholch! The names of the three beat like muffled drums in my brain. Traitors to me, Medea no less than the others, for had she not bent before the wills of Edeyrn and Matholch, had she not been willing to sacrifice me? Death I would give Edeyrn and the wolfling. Medea I might let live, but only as my slave, nothing more.

With Ghast Rhymi dead, I was leader of the Coven! In the old man's tower, sentimental weakness had nearly betrayed me. The weakness of Edward Bond, I thought. His memories had watered my will and diluted my power.

Now I no longer needed his memories. At my side swung the Crystal Mask and the Wand of Power. I knew how to get the Sword Called Llyr. It was Ganelon and not the weakling Edward Bond, who would make himself master of the Dark World.

Briefly I wondered where Bond was now. When Medea had brought me through the Need-fire to the Dark World, Edward Bond, at that moment, must have returned to Earth. I smiled ironically, imagining the surprise that must have been his. Perhaps he had tried, and was still trying, to get back to the Dark World. But without Freydis to aid him, his attempts would be useless. Freydis was helping me now, not Bond.

And Bond would stay on Earth! The substitution would not occur again if I could help it. And I *could* help it. Strong Freydis might be, but could she stand against the man who had killed Llyr? I did not think so.

I sent a sly sidewise glance at Lorryn. Fool! Arles too was another of the same breed. Only Freydis had sense enough not to trust me.

The strongest of my enemies must die first—Llyr. Then the Coven. After that, the woodsmen would taste my power. They would learn, that I was Ganelon, not the Earth weakling, Edward Bond!

I thrust the memories of Bond out of my mind. I drove them away. I banished them utterly.

As Ganelon I would battle Llyr.

And as Ganelon I would rule the Dark World!

Rule—with iron and fire!

Hours before we came to Caer Llyr we saw it, at first a blacker blackness against the night sky, and slowly, gradually, deepening into an ebon mountain as the rose-gray dawn spread behind us.

Our cantering shadows fell before us, to be trodden under the horses' hoofs. Cool, fresh winds whispered—whispered of the sacrifice at Caer Sécaire, of the seeking minds of the Coven that spied across the land.

But Caer Llyr loomed on the edge of darkness ahead—guarding the night!

Huge the Caer was, and alien. It seemed shapeless, a Titan mound of jumbled black rock thrown almost casually together. Yet I knew that there was design in its strange geometry.

Two jet pillars, each fifty feet tall, stood like the legs of a colossus, and between them was an unguarded portal. Only there was there any touch of color about the Caer.

A veil of flickering rainbow played lambently, like a veil across that threshold. Opalescent and faintly glowing, the shadow-curtain swung and quivered as though gentle winds drifted through gossamer folds of silk.

Fifty feet high was that curtain and twenty feet broad. Straddling it the ebon pillars rose. And above and beyond, towering breathtakingly to the dawn-clouded sky, squatted the Caer, a mountain-like structure that had never been built by man.

From Caer Llyr a breath of fear came coldly, scattering the woodsmen like leaves before a gale. They broke ranks, deployed out and drew together again as I raised my hand and Lorryn called a command.

I stared around the low hills surrounding us.

"Never in my memory or my father's memory have men come this close to Caer Llyr," Lorryn said. "Except for Covenanters, of course. Nor would the foresters follow me now, Bond. They follow you."

How far would they follow? My wondering thought was cut off as a woodsman shouted warning. He rose in his stirrups and pointed south.

Over the hills, riding like demons in a dusty cloud, came horsemen, their armor glittering in the red sunlight!

"So someone did escape from the Castle," I said between my teeth. "And the Coven have been warned, after all!"

Lorryn grinned and shrugged. "Not many."

"Enough to delay us." I frowned, trying to make the best plan. "Lorryn, stop them. If the Coven ride with their guards, kill them too. But hold them back from the Caer until—"

"Until?"

"I don't know. I'll need time. How much time I can't say. Battling and conquering Llyr won't be the work of a moment."

"Nor is it the work of one man," Lorryn said doubtfully. "With us to aid you, victory will fly at your elbow."

"I know the weapon against Llyr," I said. "One man can wield it. But keep the guardsmen back, and the Covenanters too. Give me time!"

"There will be no difficulty about that," Lorryn said, a flash of excitement lighting his eyes. "For look!"

Angling across the hills, riding one by one into view, hotly pursuing the armored rout, came green-clad figures, spurring their horses forward.

Those figures were woodsmen's women whom we had left behind in the valley. They were armed now, for I saw the glitter of swords. Nor were swords their only weapons. A spiteful crack echoed, a puff of smoke arose, and one of the guardsmen flung up his hands and toppled from his mount.

Edward Bond had known how to make rifles! And the woodsfolk had learned how to use them!

At the head of the woodswomen I noted two lithe forms, one a slim, supple girl whose ashy-blond hair streamed behind her like a banner. Arles.

And at her side, on a great white steed, rode one whose giant form I could not mistake even from this distance. Freydis spurred forward like a Valkyrie galloping into battle.

Freydis and Arles, and the women of the forest!

Lorryn's laugh held exultation.

"We have them Bond!" he cried, his fist tightening on the rein. "Our women at their heels, and we strike from the flank—we'll catch and crush them between hammer and anvil. Gods grant the shape-changer rides there!"

"Then ride," I snapped. "No more talk! Ride and crush them. Hold them back from the Caer!"

With that I raced my steed forward, lying low on the horse's mane, driving like a thunderbolt toward the black mountain ahead. Did Lorryn know how suicidal might be the mission on which I had sent him? Matholch he might slay, and even Medea. But if Edeyrn rode with the Coven guards, if ever she dropped the hood from her face, neither sword nor bullet could save the woodsmen!

Still they would give me time. And if the woodmen's ranks were thinned, so much the better for later. I would deal with Edeyrn in my own way when the time came.

Ahead the black columns stood. Behind me a shouting rose, and a crackle of rifle-fire. I looked back, but a fold of the hills hid the combat from my eyes.

I sprang from the horse's back and stood before the pillars— between them. The coruscating veil sparkled and ran like milky water before me. Above, towering monstrously, stood the Caer, the focus of the evil that had spread across the Dark World.

And in it reposed Llyr, my enemy!

I still had the sword I had taken from one of the woodsmen, but I doubted if ordinary steel would be much good within the Caer. Nevertheless I made sure the weapon was at my side as I walked forward.

I stepped through the veil.

For twenty paces I moved forward in utter darkness. Then light came.

But it was the light that beats upon a snow plain, so bright, so glittering, that it blinds. I stood motionless, waiting. Presently the dazzle resolved itself into flickering atoms of brightness, weaving and darting in arabesque patterns. Not cold, no!

Tropical warmth beat upon me.

The shining atoms drove at me. They tingled upon my face and hands. They sank like intangible things through my garments and were absorbed by my skin. They did not lull me. Instead, my body greedily drank that weird snowstorm of—energy?—and was in turn energized by it.

Tide of life sang ever stronger in my veins.

I saw three gray shadows against the white. Two tall and one slight and small as a child's shadow.

I knew them. I knew who cast them.

I heard Matholch's voice.

"Kill him. Kill him now."

And Medea's answer.

"No. He need not die. He must not."

"But he must!" Matholch snarled, and Edeyrn's sexless, thin voice echoed his.

"He is dangerous, Medea. He must die, and only on Llyr's altar can he be slain. For he is the Sealed of Llyr."

"He need not die," Medea said stubbornly. "If he is made harmless—weaponless —he may live."

"How?" Edeyrn asked, and for answer the red witch stepped forward out of the dazzling white shimmer.

No longer a shadow. No longer a two-dimensional grayness. She stood before me—Medea, witch of Colchis.

Her dark hair fell to her knees. Her dark gaze slanted at me. Evil she was, and alluring as Lilith.

I dropped my hand to sword-hilt.

I did not. I could not move. Faster swirled the darting bright atoms, whirling about me, sinking into my body to betray me.

I could not move.

Beyond Medea the twin shadows bent forward.

"The power of Llyr holds him," Edeyrn whispered. "But Ganelon is strong, Medea. If he breaks his fetters, we are lost."

"By then he will have no weapons," Medea said, and smiled at me.

Now indeed I knew my danger. Very easily my steel could have bitten through Medea's soft throat, and heartily I wished it had done so long ago. For I remembered Medea's power. The mutation that set her apart from the others. That which had caused her to be named—vampire.

I remembered victims of hers that I had seen. The dead-eyed guardsmen, the Castle slaves, hollow shells of men, the walking dead, all soul drained from them, and most of their life-forms as well.

Her arms stole around my neck. Her mouth lifted to mine.

In one hand she held her black wand. It touched my head, and a gentle shock, not unpleasant, crawled along my scalp. The— the conductor, I knew, and a gust of insane laughter shook me at the incongruity of the weapon.

But there was no magic here. There was science, of a high order, a science made possible only for those who were trained to it, or for those who were mutants. Medea drank energy, but not through sorcery. I had seen that wand used too often to believe that.

The wand opened and closed circuits of the mind and its energies. It tapped the brain, as a copper wire can tap a generated current.

Diverting the life-force to Medea!

The shining mist-motes swirled faster. They closed in around us, bathing us in a swirling cloak. The gray shadowiness fell away from Edeyrn and Matholch. Dun-cloaked, cowled dwarf and lean, grinning wolfling stood there, watching.

Edeyrn's face I could not see, though the deadly cold crept from beneath the cowl like an icy wind. Matholch's tongue crept out and circled his lips. His eyes were bright with triumph and excitement.

A numbing, lethargic languor was stealing over me. Against my mouth as Medea's lips grew hotter, more ardent, as my own lips chilled. Desperately I tried to move, to grasp my sword-hilt.

I could not.

Now the bright veil thinned again. Beyond Matholch and Edeyrn I could see a vast space, so enormous that my gaze failed to pierce its violet depths. A stairway led up to infinite heights.

A golden glow burned high above.

But behind Matholch and Edeyrn, a little to one side, stood a curiously-carved pedestal whose front was a single pane of transparent glass. It shone steadily with a cool blue light. What lay within I did not know, but I recognized that crystal pane.

Ghast Rhymi had spoken of it. Behind it must lie the Sword Called Llyr.

Faintly now—faintly—I heard Matholch's satisfied chuckle.

"Ganelon, my love, do not struggle against me," Medea whispered. "Only I can save you. When your madness passes we will return to the Castle."

Yes, for I would be no menace then. Matholch would not bother to harm me. As a mindless, soulless thing I would return to the Castle of the Coven as Medea's slave.

I, Ganelon, hereditary Lord of the Coven and the Sealed of Llyr!

The golden glow high above brightened. Crooked lightnings rushed out from it and were lost in the violet dimness.

My eyes found that golden light that was the Window of Llyr.

My mind reached out toward it.

My soul strained to it!

Witch and vampire-mutation Medea might be—or sorceress— but she had never been sealed to Llyr. No dark power beat latently in her blood as it beat in mine. Well I knew now that, no matter how I might renounce my allegiance to Llyr, there yet had been a bond. Llyr had power over me, but I could draw upon his power as well!

I drew on that power now!

The golden window brightened. Again forked lightnings ran out from it and were gone. A muffled, heavy drum-beat muttered from somewhere, like the pulse of Llyr.

Like the heart of Llyr, stirring from sleep to waking.

Through me power rushed, quickening my flesh from its lethargy. I drew on Llyr's power without measuring the cost. I saw fear flash across Matholch's face, and Edeyrn made a quick gesture.

"Medea," she said.

But Medea had already sensed that quickening. I felt her body quiver convulsively against mine. Avidly she pressed against me, faster and faster she drank the energy that made me alive.

But the energy of Llyr poured into me! Hollow thunders roared in the vast spaces above. The golden window blazed with dazzling brightness. And around us now the sparkling motes of light paled, shrank, and were gone.

"Kill him!" Matholch howled. "He holds Llyr!"

He sprang forward.

From somewhere a bloody figure in dented armor stumbled. I saw Lorryn's scarred face twist in amazement as he blinked at the tableau. His sword, red to the hilt, was bare in his hand.

He saw me with Medea's arms about my neck.

He saw Edeyrn.

And he saw Matholch!

A wordless, inarticulate sound ripped from Lorryn's throat. He lifted high the sword.

As I tore myself free from Medea's grip, as I sent her reeling away, I saw Matholch's wand come up. I reached for my own wand, but there was no need.

Lorryn's blade sang. Matholch's hand, still gripping the wand, was severed at the wrist. Blood spurted from cut arteries.

Howling, the shape-changer dropped forward. The lycan-thropic change came upon him. Hypnotism, mutation, dark sorcery—I could not tell. But the thing that sprang at Lorryn's throat was not human.

Lorryn laughed. He sent his sword spinning away.

He met the wolfling's charge, bracing himself strongly and caught the thing by throat and leg. Fanged jaws snapped viciously at him.

Lorryn heaved the monster above his head. His joints cracked with the inhuman strain. One instant Lorryn stood there, holding his enemy high, while the wolf-jaws snarled and strove to rend him.

He dashed the wolf down upon the stones!

I heard bones snap like rotten twigs. I heard a scream of dying, terrible agony from a gaping muzzle from which blood poured.

Then Matholch, in his own shape, broken, dying, lay writhing at our feet!

Miraculously the weakness that had chained me was gone. Llyr's strength poured through me. I unsheathed my sword and ran past Matholch's body, ignoring Lorryn who stood motionless, staring down. I ran to the pedestal with its blue-litten pane.

I gripped the sword's blade and sent the heavy hilt crashing against the glass.

It had been part of the window. For within the hollow pedestal was nothing at all. The sword had been part of the pane, so that my breaking the crystal had released the weapon from its camouflaged hiding-place.

Along the sleek blade blue light ran. Within the crystal blue fires burned wanly. I bent and picked up the sword. The hilt was warm and alive.

The Sword Called Llyr in my left hand, the sword with blade of steel in my right, I stood upright.

Paralyzing cold breathed past me.

I knew that cold.

So I did not turn. I swung the steel sword under my arm, snatching the Crystal Mask from my belt, and donned it. I drew the Wand of Power.

Only then did I turn.

Through the Mask queer glimmers and shiftings ran, distorting what I saw. The properties of light were oddly altered by the Mask. But it had its purpose. It was a filter.

Matholch lay motionless now. Beyond his body Medea was rising to her feet, her dark hair disordered. Facing me stood Lorryn, a stone man, only his eyes alive in his set, white face.

He was staring at Edeyrn, whose sleek dark head I saw. Her back was toward me. The cowl had been flung back upon her shoulders.

Lorryn sagged down, the life going out of him. Bonelessly as water he collapsed.

He lay dead.

Then, slowly, slowly, Edeyrn turned.

She was tiny as a child, and her face was like a child's too, in its immature roundness. But I did not see her face, for even through the Crystal Mask burned the Gorgon's glare.

The blood stilled within me. A slow tide of ice crept with iron lethargy into my brain and cold wariness engulfed me.

Only in the eyes of the Gorgon fire burned.

Deadly radiations were there, what Earth-scientists call ectogenetic rays, but limited till now to the plant-world. Only the mad mutation that had created Edeyrn could have brought from hell such a nightmare trick of biology.

But I did not fall. I did not die. The radiations were filtered, made harmless, by the vibration-warping properties of the Mask I wore.

I lifted the Wand of Power.

Red fires blasted from it. Scarlet, licking tongues seared out toward Edeyrn.

Lashes of flames tore at her, like crimson whips that burned and left bloody weals on that calm child-face.

She drew back, the lance of her stare driving at me.

With her, step by step, retreated Medea. Toward the foot of the great stairway that led to Llyr's Window.

The whips of fire seared across her eyes.

She turned and, stumbling, began to run up the stairway. Medea paused, her arms lifted in an uncompleted gesture. But in my face she read no softening.

She, too, turned, and followed Edeyrn.

I dropped the useless sword of steel. Wand in left hand, the Sword Called Llyr in my right, I followed them.

As my foot touched the first step, a trembling vibration shook the violet air about me. Now almost I regretted having called upon Llyr to break Medea's spell. For Llyr was awake, watching, and warned.

The pulse of Llyr muttered through the huge Caer. The golden lightnings flamed from the Window high above.

Briefly two black small silhouettes showed against that amber glow. They were Edeyrn and Medea, climbing.

After them I went. And at each step the way grew harder. I seemed to walk through a thickening, invisible torrent that was like a wind or a wave flowing down from that shining window, striving to tear me from my foothold, to rip the crystal sword from my grip.

Up and up I went. Now the Window was a glaring blaze of yellow fires. The lightnings crackled out incessantly, while rocking crashes of thunder reverberated along the vaulted abysses of the Caer. I leaned forward as though against a gale. Doggedly I fought my way up the stair.

There was someone behind me.

I did not turn. I dared not, for fear the torrent would sweep me from my place. I crawled up the last few steps, and came out on a level platform of stone, a disc-shaped dais, on which stood a ten-foot cube. Three of its sides were of black rock. The side that faced me was a glaring blaze of amber brilliance.

Far below, dizzyingly far, was the floor of the Caer. Behind me the stairway ran down to those incredible depths, and the tremendous wind still blew upon me, pouring out from the Window, seeking to whirl me to my death.

To the Window's left stood Edeyrn, to its right, Medea. And in the Window—

The blazing golden clouds whirled, thickened, tossed like storm-mists, while still the blinding flashes spurted from them. The thunder never ceased now. But it pulsed. It rose and fell in steady cadence, in unison with the heart-beat of Llyr.

Monster or mutation—human once, or half-human—Llyr had grown in power since then. Ghast Rhymi had warned me.

Part machine and part pure energy and part something un-thinkable, the power of Llyr blasted through the golden clouds upon me!

The Wand of Power dropped from my hand. I lifted the crystal sword and managed one forward step. Then the hell-tide caught me, and I could advance no further. I could only fight, with every bit of my strength, against the avalanche that strove to thrust me toward the edge of the hanging platform.

Louder grew the thunders. Brighter the lightings flamed.

The cold stare of Edeyrn chilled me. Medea's face was inhuman now. Yellow clouds boiled out from the Window and caught Edeyrn and Medea in their embrace.

Then they rolled toward me and overwhelmed me.

Dimly I could see the brighter glow that marked Llyr's Window. And two vague silhouettes, Edeyrn and Medea.

I strove to step forward. Instead I was borne back toward the edge—back and back.

Great arms caught me about the waist. A braid of white hair tossed by my eyes. The giant strength of Freydis stood like a wall of iron between me and the abyss.

From the corner of my eyes I saw that she had wound a scrap torn from her white robe about her head, shielding her from the Gorgon's stare. Blindly, guided by some strange instinct, the Valkyrie thrust me forward.

Against us the golden clouds rolled, sentient, palpable, veined with white lightnings and shaking with deep thunders.

Freydis strove silently. I bent forward like a bow, battering against the torrent.

Step by step I won forward, Freydis to aid me. Ever she stood as a bulwark against my back. I could hear her panting breath, great gasps that ripped from her throat as she linked her strength with mine.

My chest felt as though a white-hot core of iron was driven through it. Yet I went on. Nothing existed now but that golden brightening amid the clouds, clouds of creation, sentient with the shaking tumult of breaking universes, worlds beyond worlds crashing into ruin under the power of Llyr . . ..

I stood before the Window.

Without volition my arm swept up. I brought the Sword Called Llyr smashing down upon Llyr's Window.

In my hand the sword broke.

It fell to tinkling fragments at my feet. The veined blue glimmers writhed and coiled about the broken blade.

Were sucked into the Window.

Back rushed the cloud-masses. A tremendous, nearly unbearable vibration ripped through the Caer, shaking it like a sapling. The golden clouds were drawn through the Window.

With them went Edeyrn and Medea!

One glimpse I had of them, the brand of my fire like a red mask across Edeyrn's eyes, Medea's face despairing and filled with a horror beyond life, her gaze fixed on me with an imploring plea that was infinitely terrible. Then they vanished!

For one instant I saw through the Window. I saw something beyond space and time and dimension, a writhing, ravening chaos that bore down upon Medea and Edeyrn and a golden core of light that I knew for Llyr.

Once almost human, Llyr, at the end, bore no relation to anything remotely human.

The grinding millstones of Chaos crushed the three!

The thunder died.

Before me stood the altar of Llyr. But it held no Window, now. All four sides were of black, dead stone!

Blackness and black stones were the last things I saw, before dark oblivion closed down over me like folding wings. It was as if Llyr's terrible resistance was all that had held me upright in the last fierce stages of our struggle. As he fell, so fell Ganelon at the foot of the Windowless altar.

How long I lay there I do not know. But slowly, slowly Caer Llyr came back around me, and I knew I was lying prostrate upon the altar. I sat up painfully, the dregs of exhaustion still stiffening my body, though I knew I must have slept, for that exhaustion was no longer the overwhelming tide that had flooded me as I fell.

Beyond me, at the head of the great steep of stairs, Freydis lay, half stretched upon the steps as if she had striven to return to her people in the moment before collapsing. Her eyes were still bound, and her mighty arms lay flung out upon the platform, all strength drained from them by the fierceness of our battle. Strangely, as she lay there, she brought back to my double-minded memories the thought of a figure from Earth—another mighty woman in white robes, with bandaged eyes and upraised arms, blind Justice holding her eternal scales. Faintly I smiled at the thought. In the Dark World—my world, now—Justice was Ganelon, and not blind.

Freydis stirred. One hand lifted uncertainly to the cloth across her eyes. I let her waken. Presently we must struggle again together, Justice and I. But I did not doubt who would prevail.

I rose to my knees, and heard a silvery tinkling as something slid in fragments from my shoulder. The Mask, broken when I fell. Its crystal shards lay among those other shards which had blasted Llyr from the Dark World when the Sword broke. I thought of the strange blue lightnings which had wrought at last what no other thing in the Dark World could accomplish—Llyr's destruction. And I thought I understood.

He had passed too far beyond this world ever to touch it except in the ceremonies of the Golden Window. Man, demon, god, mutation into namelessness—whatever he had been, he had kept but one link with the Dark World which spawned him. A link enshrined in the Sword Called

Llyr. By that talisman he could return for the sacrifices which fed him, return for the great ceremonies of the Sealing that had made me half his own. But only by that talisman.

So it must be safely hidden to be his bridge for the returning. And safely hidden it was. Without Ghast Rhymi's knowledge, who could have found it? Without the strength of the great Lord Ganelon—well, yes, and the strength of Freydis too—who could have won close enough to the window to shatter the Sword upon the only thing in the Dark World that would break it? Yes, Llyr had guarded his talisman as strongly as any guard could be. But vulnerable he was, to the one man who could wield that Sword.

So the Sword broke, and the bridge between worlds broke, and Llyr was gone into a chaos from which there could never be a returning.

Medea, too—red witch of Colchis, lost love, drinker of life, gone beyond recalling . . ..

For a moment I closed my eyes.

"Well, Ganelon?"

I looked up. Freydis was smiling grimly at me from beneath the uplifted blindfold. I rose to my feet and watched in silence while she got to hers. Triumph flooded through me in great waves of intoxicating warmth. The world I had just wakened to was wholly mine now, and not this woman or any other human should balk me of my destiny. Had I not vanquished Llyr and slain the last of the Coven? And was I not stronger in magic than any man or woman now who walked the Dark World? I laughed, the deep sound echoing from the high vaults about us and rolling back in reverberant exultation until that which had been Caer Llyr was alive with the noise of my mirth. But Llyr was here no longer.

"Let this be Caer Ganelon!" I said, hearing the echo of my own name come rolling back as if the castle itself replied.

"Ganelon!" I shouted. "Caer Ganelon!" I laughed to hear the whole vast hollow repeating my name. While the echoes still rolled I spoke to Freydis.

"You have a new master now, you forest people! Because you helped me you shall be rewarded, old woman, but I am master of the Dark World—I Ganelon!" And the walls roared back to me, "Ganelon—Ganelon!"

Freydis smiled.

"Not so fast, Covenanter," she said calmly. "Did you think I trusted you?"

I gave her a scornful smile. "What can you do to me now? Only one thing could slay me before today—Llyr Himself. Now Llyr is gone, and Ganelon is immortal! You have no power to touch me, sorceress!"

She straightened on the step, her ageless face a little below mine. There was a sureness in her eyes that sent the first twinge of uneasiness into my mind. Yet what I had said was true for no one in the Dark World could harm me, now. Yet Freydis' smile did not waver.

"Once I sent you through limbo into the Earth World," she said. "Could you stop me if I sent you there again?"

Relief quieted my tremor of unease.

"Tomorrow or the next day—yes, I could stop you. Today, no. But I am Ganelon now, and I know the way back. I am Ganelon, and forewarned, and I think you could not so easily send me Earthward again, naked of memories and clothed in another man's past. I remember and I could return. You would waste your time and mine, Freydis. Yet try it, if you will and I warn you, I should be back again before your spell was finished."

Her quiet smile did not falter. She folded her arms, hiding her hands in the flowing sleeves. She was very sure of herself.

"You think you are a godling, Ganelon," she said. "You think no mortal power can touch you now. You have forgotten one thing. As Llyr had his weakness, as Edeyrn did, and Medea and Matholch so have you, Covenanter. In this world there is no man to match you. But in the Earth World there is, Lord Ganelon! In that world your equal lives, and I mean to call him out to fight one last battle for the freedom of the Dark World. Edward Bond could slay you, Ganelon!"

I felt the blood leave my face, a little wind of chill like Edeyrn's glance breathed over me. I *had* forgotten. Even Llyr, by his own unimaginable hand, could have died. And I could die by my own hand too, or by the hand of that other self who was Edward Bond.

"Fool!" I said. "Dotard! Have you forgotten that Bond and I can never stand in the same world? When I came, he vanished out of this land, just as I must vanish if you bring him here. How can a man and his reflection ever come hand to hand? How could he touch me, old woman?"

"Easily," she smiled. "Very easily. He cannot fight you here, nor in the Earth World that is true. But limbo, Ganelon? Have you forgotten limbo?"

Her hands came out of her sleeves. There was a road of blinding silver in each. Before I could stir she had brought the rods together, crossing them before her smiling face. At the intersection forces of tremendous power blazed into an instant's being, forces that streamed from the poles of the world and could touch only for the beat of a second if that world were not to be shaken into fragments. I felt the building reel below me.

I felt the gateway open.

Here was grayness, nothing but oblivion made visible all around me. I staggered with the suddenness of it, the shock, and the terrible tide of anger that came surging up through my whole body at the knowledge of Freydis' trickery. It was not to be endured, this magicking of the Dark World's lord! I would fight my way back, and the vengeance I would wreak upon Freydis would be a lesson to all.

Out of the greyness a mirror loomed before me. A mirror? I saw my own face, bewildered, uncomprehending, staring back into my eyes. But I was not wearing the ragged blue garments of sacrifice which I had donned so many aeons ago in the Castle of the Coven. I seemed to wear Earth garments, and I seemed not quite myself, not quite Ganelon. I seemed—

"Edward Bond!" said the voice of Freydis behind me.

The reflection of myself glanced across my shoulder, and a look of recognition and unutterable relief came over it.

"Freydis!" he cried, in my own voice. "Freydis, thank God! I've tried so hard—"

"Wait," Freydis stopped him. "Listen. There is one last trial before you. This man is Ganelon. He has undone all your work among the forest people. He has slain Llyr and the Coven. There is none in the Dark World to stay his hand if he wins his way back to it. Only you can stop him, Edward Bond. Only you."

I did not wait for her to say anything more. I knew what must be done. I lunged forward before he could speak or stir, and drove a heavy blow into the face that might have been my own. It was a strange thing to do. It was a hard thing. At the last moment my muscles almost refused me, for it was as if I struck myself.

I saw him reel back, and my own head reeled in imagination, so that the first blow rocked us both.

He caught himself a dozen feet away and stood for a moment, unsteady on his feet, looking at me with confusion that might have been the mirror of my own face, for I knew there was confusion there too.

Then anger flushed those bewildering, familiar features, and I saw blood break from the corner of his mouth and trickle across his chin. I laughed savagely. That blood, somehow, made him my enemy. I had seen the blood of enemies, springing out in the wake of my blows, too often to mistake him now for anything but what he was. Myself—and my deadliest foe.

He dropped into a half-crouch and came for me, stooping to protect his body from my fists. I wished fervently for a sword or a gun. I have never cared for an equal fight, as Ganelon does not fight for sport, but to win. But this fight must be terribly, unbelievably equal.

He dodged beneath my blow, and I felt the rocking jar of what seemed to be my own fist jolting against my cheekbone. He danced back, light-footed, out of range.

Rage came snarling up in my throat. I wanted nothing of this boxing, this game fought by rules. Ganelon fought to win! I roared at him from the full depth of my lungs and hurled myself forward in a crushing embrace that carried us both heavily to the gray sponginess that was limbo's floor. My fingers sank delightfully in his throat. I groped savagely for his eyes. He grunted with effort and I felt his fist thud into my ribs, and felt the sharp white pain of breaking bone.

So wholly was he myself, and I he, that for an instant I was not sure whose rib had snapped beneath whose blow. Then I drew a deep breath and sobbed it out again half finished as pain like bright light flashed through my body, and I knew it was my own rib.

The knowledge maddened me. Careless of pain or caution, I drove my fists savagely into him at blind random, feeling exultantly the crackle of bone beneath my knuckles, the spurt of blood over my hard-clenched hands. We stove together in a terrible locked embrace, there upon the floor of limbo, in a nightmare that had no real being, except for the pain shooting through me after each breath.

But in a moment or two, I knew somehow, very surely, that I was his master. And this is how I knew. He rolled half over to jab a hard blow into my face, and before the blow began, I had blocked it. I had *known*. He squirmed from beneath me and braced himself to strike me again in the ribs, and before he could strike, I had twisted sidewise away. Again I had *known*.

For I had been Edward Bond once, in every way that matters. I had lived in his memory and his world. And I knew Edward Bond as I knew myself. Instinct seemed to tell me what he would do next. He could not out-think me, and so he could not hope to out-fight me, to whom his every thought was revealed in the moment before he could act upon it.

Even in the pain of my broken rib, I laughed then. Freydis had overreached herself at last! In smothering Ganelon under Edward Bond's memories in the Earth World, she had given me the means to vanquish him now! He was mine, to finish when I chose, and the Dark World was mine, and Edward Bond's kingdom of free people was mine too, and Edward Bond's lovely pale-haired bride, and everything that might have been his own.

I laughed exultantly, and twisted in three perfectly timed motions that blocked and overbalanced the man who was myself. Three motions only—and then I had him across my knee, taut-stretched, his spine pressing hard against my thigh.

I grinned down at him. My blood dripped into his face. I saw it strike there, and I met his eyes, and then strangely, for one flashing instant, I knew a fierce yearning for defeat. In that instant, I prayed voicelessly to a nameless god that Edward Bond might yet save himself, and Ganelon might die . . ..

I called forth all the strength that was in me, and limbo swam redly before my eyes and the pain of my broken rib was a lance of white light as I drew the deep breath that was Edward Bond's last.

I broke his back across my knee.

Hurriedly two cold, smooth hands pressed hard upon my forehead. I looked up. They slid lower, covering my eyes. And weakness was like a blanket over me. I knelt there, unresisting, feeling the body of the man who had been myself slide limply from my knee.

Freydis pressed me down. We lay side by side, the living and the dead.

The silver rods of the sorceress touched my head, and made a bridge between Edward Bond and Ganelon. I remembered Medea's wand that could draw the life-force from the mind. A dull, numbing paralysis had me. Little tingling shocks rippled through my nerves, and I could not move.

Sudden agonizing pain shot through me. My back! I tried to scream with the white fury of that wrenching agony, but my throat was frozen. I felt Edward Bond's wounds!

In that nightmare moment, while my brain spun down the limitless corridors of a science beyond that of mankind, I knew what Freydis had done—what she was doing.

I felt the mind of Edward Bond come back from the gulfs. Side by side we lay in flesh, and side by side in spirit as well.

There was blackness, and two flames, burning with a cold, clear fire . . ..

One was the mind—the life—of Edward Bond. One was my life!

The flames bent toward each other!

They mingled and were one!

Life and soul and mind of Edward Bond merged with life of Ganelon!

Where two flames had burned, there was one now. One only.

And the identify of Ganelon, ebbed, sank . . .faded into a graying shadow as the fires of Edward Bond's life leaped ever higher!

We were one. We were—

Edward Bond! No longer Ganelon! No longer Lord of the Dark World, Master of the Caers!

Magic of Freydis drowned the soul of Ganelon and gave his body to the life of Edward Bond!

I saw Ganelon—*die!*. . .

When I opened my eyes again, I knelt upon the altar that had been Llyr's. The empty vaults towered hollowly above us. Limbo was gone. The body across my knee was gone. Freydis smiled down at me with her ageless, timeless smile.

"Welcome back to the Dark World, Edward Bond."

Yes, it was true. I knew that. I knew my own identity, housed though it was in another man's body. Dizzily I blinked, shook my head, and rose slowly. Pain struck savagely at my side, and I gasped and let Freydis spring forward to support me on one great white arm, while the hollow building reeled about me. But Ganelon was gone. He had vanished with limbo, vanished like a scatter of smoke, vanished as if the prayer he breathed in his extremity had been answered by the nameless god he prayed to.

I was Edward Bond again.

"Do you know why Ganelon could break you, Edward Bond?" Freydis said softly. "Do you know why you could not vanquish him? It was not what he thought. I know he believed he read your mind because he had dwelt there, but that was not the reason. When a man fights himself, my son, the same man does not fight to win. Only the suicide hates himself. Deep within Ganelon lay the knowledge of his own evil, and the hatred of it. So he could strike his own image and exult in the blow, because he hated himself in the depths of his own mind.

"But you had earned your own respect. You could not strike as hard as he because you are not evil. And Ganelon won—and lost. In the end, he did not fight me. He had slain himself, and the man who does that has no combat left in him."

Her voice sank to a murmur. Then she laughed.

"Go out now, Edward Bond. There is much to be done in the Dark World!"

So, leaning upon her arm, I went down the long steps that Ganelon had climbed. I saw the green glimmer of the day outside, the shimmer of leaves, the motion of waiting people. I remembered all that Ganelon had remembered, but upon the mind of Ganelon the mind of Edward Bond was forever superimposed, and I knew that only thus could the Dark World be ruled.

The two together, twinned forever in one body, and the control forever mine—Edward Bond's.

We came out under the emptied arch of the opening, and daylight was blinding for a moment after that haunted darkness. Then I saw the foresters anxiously clustering in their battered ranks around the Caer, and I saw a pale girl in green, haloed by her floating hair, turn a face of incredulous radiance to mine.

I forgot the pain in my side.

Arles' hair swam like mist about us both as my arms closed around her. The roar of exultation that went up from the forest people swept the clearing and made the great Caer behind us echo through all its hollow vaults.

The Dark World was free, and ours.

But, Medea, Medea, red witch of Colchis, how we might have reigned together.